T0328752

Bhlawa's Inconsolable Spirits

2023© Mxolisi Nyezwa

ISBN 978-1-928476-48-1
ebook ISBN 978-1-928476-49-8

Deep South, Makhanda
contact@deepsouth.co.za
www.deepsouth.co.za

Distributed in South Africa by
Blue Weaver Marketing and Distribution
https://blueweaver.co.za

Distributed worldwide by
African Books Collective
PO Box 721, Oxford, OX1 9EN, UK
www.africanbookscollective.com/publishers/deep-south

Deep South would like to thank the National Arts Council
for financially supporting the production of this book

Cover art: Cyprian Shilakoe, *Mma Koko* (1971), Etching on paper
Collection: Durban Art Gallery
Photographed by Roy Reed

Cover design: JMS Design
Text design and layout: Liz Gowans

Bhlawa's Inconsolable Spirits

Mxolisi Nyezwa

1

From quite an early age I could never forgive the earth for planting a fidgety tree of imagination and questions inside my head. My first despair came with the sad realization that nothing grew in our home back garden. The weary maize plants that my father planted petered out swiftly without yield.

Before I could even complete kindergarten, the chessboard of all the rooks, pawns, bishops, knights, kings and queens that would eventually impact my life was introduced to me. What happens to you later in life is merely a reminder or replay of what you went through or experienced, which was shown to you earlier by the birds. You were alive in your infancy. The world doesn't tell you that. But the birds know. All planets wake up each morning like the red sun from a galaxy of weary stars and journey to us. Our adult lives are terrible dreams. At Kama Lower Primary school where my parents first sent me to learn about the things of the world, I met everyone who I was going to meet in my life, saw everything else that was going to happen to me.

I am now convinced that the little that I remember, which isn't even a quarter of my childhood, is the significant portion of a life that I must always remember. The blurred snapshots my memory has erased, or kept so far back that I can no longer retrieve them, will perhaps become significant in another life that I will live somewhere far away, in another world.

My parents told me that when they first arrived in Bhlawa there were no street lights or water in the taps. Uko, the crying spirit, roamed the streets during the freezing nights. Township people followed the dusty streets right to where they disappeared on the horizon. They called the end of their world eMpelazwe. Beyond that invisible demarcation line of apartheid lay the white man's vast empire, the big city of Port Elizabeth, with its defiant statue of an English woman, Queen Victoria, overlooking the dizzy waters of the sleeping bay. From another angle she is turning her back against the Main Library building that stands packed with jobless black students and workers reading the *Evening Post*, always on the look out for jobs in the bone-dry economy of the city.

Bhlawa people were poor. The streets were a thousand prisons that were laughing at our poverty. The cramped buildings that lined these opaque streets were orange or green in colour like hospitals. Melancholy surrounded the churches. Old women carried their poor men's overalls with exaggerated fury. In the 80's the township was a sanctuary for the comrades who crept in under the dark blanket of night to prepare the way for an insurrection against the illegitimate white government. The National Party government put into law midnight curfews, the state of emergency and other diabolical laws that restricted the movement of the poor residents. South Africa was being led off to its place of execution by a small group of frightened white men. I felt confident that gradually sanity would set in, and over time South Africa's history would be washed clean of arsenal blood. I had seen enough of the brutality of life. All of us continued the dazzling dream of an impostor, pretending that history or fate would atone for our crimes. The government repaid by killing more freedom fighters.

I emerged from our dark and unpainted bedrooms in Madala Street at night and entered our living room with its one centre-light in the ceiling doggedly brightening up the space. On the walls the photos of our dear departed family ancestors were seen more clearly, and the paths and reasons for the lives we lived were openly revealed and became understood. I was slowly seeing with innocent eyes that in the bigger scheme of things in Bhlawa I was smaller and less significant than a dead flower. Inside the body of the human the spirit of the angel child is blindfolded by unfolding events. Angels are only totally happy outside in the atmosphere like the birds, in a free life away from the tiring wanderings and conversations of humans. That is when the star angels inside us regain their heavenly powers to foretell the future and live eternally without fears of the sounds of the oceans or drowning.

2

Bhlawa – New Brighton township – where I was born in 1967, was a distasteful place of crime and violent men, a murderous world that my soul yearned desperately to escape, a place of light-footed conspiracies, with people who bowed to violins and the mean-spirited orchestra of the soldiers. And there was always the threat of the overzealous izibonda, district councillors who bullied the community and sent trespassers without valid passes back to the rural areas.

I went out in the night to buy Van Ryn's cigarettes for my father. In my two eyes I saw approaching the bitter steps of the moon. I believed that the sun came out of caves in the western hemisphere. Each morning the sky flew like a bird of prey towards Bhlawa from a broken plate on a small planet. Nothing was straight or fair. What everybody saw up there at night in Bhlawa, and called the moon, was just the hungry face of God. As children we were always taught to be wary of the sky. People believed that God's heaven was in the clouds.

I have lived in Bhlawa all my life, from the day or night I was born in Madala Street. For 33 years I lived in my parents' house. For the 21 years since then, I have lived in a flat made of red bricks in Ntshekisa Street, a few metres away from the three-roomed house in Madala which I called my home. I've visited different places in the world – towns, rural homesteads, big cities, but never for too long, and very rarely. But rather, like a ship that is hauled with

8

long ropes over a treacherous sea to a deserted bay, I have been moored to this singular harbour of a township that is inhabited by drowning men.

Our neighbours occupied in confusion the one spliced half of the squatting monster of a building that we called our home at 4 Madala. My family resided in the other half, with our chimneyed ten-foot kitchen with its two small windows, one in the front dining room overlooking the small yard, the second at the back dominating the miniature kitchen. Fitted somewhere in this crazy fart of a house were a condensed dining room and two tiny bedrooms, lying like drowned fishes next to each other, the one for our parents, the second for us children, a room sparse and dishevelled, dazed and bruised like a battered boxer.

My first memories as a child were images of violence and blood. Police and soldiers beating down doors and shouting out strangers' names in the nights. Next to the small spaza shop close to the bus stop in Ferguson Road, my friend Dumi played dice with the kids from the nearby railway houses.

Every day I saw the children in the streets crying their eyes out, beating hard against the torn eardrums of God. I thought nothing of charity or the Church. Very early in my young life I convinced myself to love everything that was delinquent, including the streets, stray animals, limping beggars, alcoholics, drug addicts and lonely people. I suffered because I began to learn and see more than my eyes and ears could absorb. I suffered hallucinations and endless toothaches.

Every day, after my mother left for her nursing job at the hospital, I was alone with my two brothers, Mbambeleli and Vusumzi. We shut the doors and listened to songs on Radio Bantu. We played many games. One game was to write down the words of the songs that play on Radio Bantu. The neighbours started shouting and cursing outside. By evening the lights switched on in our neighbours' houses, and still neither of our parents had returned from their jobs in the faraway city.

I was afraid of the streets of Bhlawa. Thugs and tsotsis would run riot there, as they still do, and hold the township to ransom. They struck at any hour, day and night, shattering lives and leaving a cold trail of blood. We used to crouch indoors and listen to their howls and whistles and their running feet.

"Mxolisi, did you lock the back door?"

"Yes, Tata."

"Turn off the light in the kitchen!"

"Yes, I will do so Tata."

Outside we hear a chilling cry that goes on and on relentlessly into the bitingly cold night. When I look in the mirror, the mirror plays a funny trick with my face, creating long halos and grave contours on my brow and below my two cheeks. My face is stony like a grown man. I stay up all night singing. It is hot. A little light illuminates the yard. The moth submits herself to the dragonfly. Everyone that I know mumbles and drinks themselves into a stupor. Violent poison is killing the children of the township. My father does not ride his bicycle. I try to make sense of what I hear.

"Who are they?"

"Where do they come from?"
"Did you say they took everything, including the old shops?"
"Which girl?"
"No! it is just a boy."
"Male or female?"
"No, just a small boy."

On the streets we kids played mindless happy games that built our agility. One was called snuka where a ball was thrown at one boy, who had to duck and jump all over, and speed off to reach a safe position. Another was bhadi, a girls' game, but young boys were welcome. Again the body was the target of a moving ball that was thrown by two members of the other team. The player in the middle of the field had to duck the speeding ball. The other side collected points every time the ball missed its target.

Father brought us colourful balloons to play with. We would blow the balloons until they attained the size of small moons, running wildly excited around our house with short nylon strings that kept the balloons high up in the air above our heads. We would start to dream that the good life was indeed possible, that Mother God was doing everything possible to redeem us from our sorrowful fate. The colourful balloons above our heads were our future lives scaling the big and vast Bhlawa sky on their way to better lands.

3

For thirty years my father woke up at 4 a.m. in the early morning and cycled to work in town, leaving at precisely 4.20 a.m. with a lunchbox and the padlock keys to open the gates and huge offices of the insurance company. His entire life was a labourer's hard routine of Monday to Saturday straight shifts. Only his Sundays were for his wife and his family. Otherwise his entire life belonged to the company.

My mother slaved her young years as a nurse at Livingstone Hospital. Her letter of appointment from the then acting medical superintendent at the hospital, Y. du Toit, dated 9/11/76 stated: "You are hereby appointed to a post of Sister on the establishment of this institution in a temporary capacity with effect from 1/11/76. The appointment is effected in accordance with the provisions of the Hospital Service Ordinance No. 23 of 1958 and the Regulations as amended, framed in terms of that Ordinance. Termination of your services shall be subjected to 24 hours notice in writing on either side."

My mother was then 36 years old. It took another 14 years, until 1990, when she was 50, before she was permanently employed by the hospital. The style of the form letter had changed, and the medical superintendent wrote, "Dear Mrs Nyezwa. With regard to your application for employment, I have pleasure in advising you that your appointment has been approved. A cordial welcome is extended to you and it is trusted that you will be happy in the service of the Administration."

My mother worked another ten years at Livingstone Hospital and retired in 2000 when she reached 60 (my father had already died two years earlier). She worked a twelve hour shift every day. These shifts were changed every few months. On some months she would work from seven in the morning to seven in the evening. Her next shift would then be seven in the evening to seven in the morning. Growing up, we, the males in the house including my father, always had to take turns rubbing her back, which was slowly breaking because of the hard hospital labour.

Saturdays we kids went to the downtown music shop to buy new records of our favourite musicians. I was not aware at that time how white folks despised us hunger-ravaged kids. I was always scared of white men. Something in their confident strides and the bulky swagger of their bodies warned me to keep my distance. Our father at home always told us, "We have enough food in the house, and makwedini, I don't want to see you loitering in town, begging the white people for a job." We always listened to him, me and my brothers. He was our father and we instinctively knew that something was wrong in the white town.

One day my father took me and my brothers for a picnic in dead town (as we children called the white city of Port Elizabeth). Near Humewood we sat down in a green valley facing the sea. My father laid down a blanket on the grass and carefully placed our food and drinks. We were busy chatting with one another excitedly, it was our family's first outing. All at once a police van driven by four white cops stopped just opposite where we were sitting. The big cops approached my father and spoke to him in a harsh Afrikaans accent, warning the family to immediately pack up and go from the area which was reserved for white people. My enthusiasm for God disappeared. We quickly put back our food into our picnic baskets and headed back to Bhlawa. On the bus home we were a silent bunch, with our father completely gutted from inside and refusing to say anything about the incident.

Our parents and our neighbours were workers in the white people's homes and shops, as foremen and security men, oomantshingilane in the harsh government clinics, police departments and railway stations. Very few of them owned cars. My father rode a bicycle. Every inch of their hard sweat was returned to us in the afternoons as sweets and other savoury delicacies from the shops in town. My father had a brown briefcase in which he packed small groceries – bread, eggs, fried chips, sliced polony and the *Evening Post*. He took it every day to work and opened it dramatically every evening to share the food with us. Sometimes it was fish and chips that he brought from the Chinese shops in town. During the lazy mornings on weekends, my brothers and myself would play children's games with the other kids in Madala. The streets where we played feverish games were safe avenues where we slowly learnt about the beauty and the ugliness of life.

Every house in Bhlawa had a waskom, a washbasin to wash our black skin of the dirt of apartheid. I suppose keeping our bodies clean freed us in a way from the hatred of white people. The names of Tambo and Mandela frightened our parents. Children from strict Christian homes like ours were forbidden to mention those two names. I went to church, to school or spaza shops looking all the time at the cluttered buildings in front of me. At the shops we got bhuzayz and oonothethayo sweets when we bought bread and sugar. Sweet messages like "I love you", or "Be my girlfriend" were engraved like hieroglyphics on onothethayo, the talking candies. Bhuzayz came in distinct shapes like scrawls from a drunk architect's hands. The talking candies wrought havoc in our home as our parents fought hard battles to prevent cavities in our teeth and other atrocious diseases of the gums.

We were often visited by our uncles who would ask us children to sizithuthe, recite our clan names. My father's family is of the Mabamba clan. Ukuzithutha, singing our patrilineal praises, included the recitation of ancient names of the family ancestors (on my father's side) and family totems. Our praises often went like this: "Mna ndinguMbamba, uThangana, uKrila, uBholose, uRhaso, uNqeno, uMalishe, uTshobathole kaNgqika, uMbombo, uBhodlinja ("the one who burps like a dog") ... and so on. The one who remembered and sang the most izibongo (praises) was given a pat on the back. On occasion a small gift was even offered to encourage him.

The practice of ukuzithutha transmitted our amaXhosa traditional culture and helped people to remember their clan's lineage. Ukuzithutha encouraged boys to become the custodians of their culture. I always dreaded the coming to our home of one old man, Uncle Limba, who had a horrible habit of kissing small boys on top of the head. He would almost always ask, "Ungubani kwedini?" whenever he visited, expecting us boys to identify our clan names. A wet kiss on top of the head inevitably followed the correct answer of "Thangana, Krila..." We would run away immediately, unclasping ourselves from the leering grasp of Tat' uLimba, dreading his wet alcoholic kisses on top of our heads.

4

A magisterial boundary wall sliced the back of our house in Madala Street neatly into two half-houses. Behind a shimmering wooden door there was a toilet which we shared with our neighbours. Sometimes, feeling the urge to relieve myself, I would quickly run outside with a torn page of a newspaper, only to find the toilet locked. I would wait some minutes outside, jumping up and down, trying to relax my stomach nerves. The wooden door of the toilet would just stand there, not budging. I would knock, now loudly calling out to the user inside to hurry up, but there would be no answer.

The toilet's wooden door had two vents, above and below, each the size of a tiny window. Sometimes a prankster would lock himself inside, for no clear reason, staying there inside for hours. I guess some people used the toilet for their sex meetings. You always had to look through the opening at the bottom of the toilet door to ascertain the real business of the user inside. And when crouched low enough, and peeping through the opening, your eyes would normally fall on the two large feet of the user who was sitting on the toilet seat, emptying their bowels. You would hear the loud groans as the occupant relieved their cramped stomach. Sometimes when you looked through the lower opening of the locked toilet, there would be no sign of life, no feet. And you would be mortified by the strange scene of an empty toilet that had locked itself from inside. How did this happen? How did they come out from the toilet leaving the door latched inside? This remained a mystery to us for years until someone revealed the secret. The mysterious culprit with the invisible feet had been standing on the toilet seat to hide his feet.

We found out this was Tshupi's favourite game. Tshupi loved to smoke zol. Every night when he was stoned he would bawl out loud like a donkey for the whole community to hear, shouting insult after insult to everyone in his family. Sometimes in Tshupi's drunken rants all of us in Madala Street were targets. He was a harsh poet of the black night, always dazzling the sleeping night with his curses. "Amangcwaba enu aluhlaza. Amangcwaba enu anilindile. Niza kufa nonke, omnye emva komnye. Ndinigcinele imoto encinci. Mzoxolo! Mzoxolo! Ndiyafunga uzakuhamba ujikeleze iBhlawa ngemoto encinci enamavili amabini." (Your graves are green. They are waiting for you. You will die, one after the other. I found a tiny cart for you. Mzoxolo! Mzoxolo! I swear you will drive around Bhlawa in a small car with two wheels).

I knew that trapped inside our bodies there was a spirit child, a restless angel that dared to go out from the strict confines of the human body to roam the entire world. All of us were grieving angels. Yet every one of us had learnt and imbibed the hard and sullen ways of our oppressors. That was why at night all humans in the township were consumed by nightmares. Tshupi was another fallen angel, a restless soul child who had fallen into a bottomless human body. Mzoxolo, the neighbourhood boy who Tshupi had been cursing, had turned notoriously bad in his ways, robbing people and delivery vehicles that drove to Bhlawa. His life of crime ended after a violent shootout with the police in one of his attempted robberies when he was shot

18

and badly injured in the spine, and became paralysed from the waist down.

Tshupi never bothered to improve his character or abandon his habits, even though he was punished every time after misbehaving. He was the sweetest person in the world when he was sober, with a lovely singing voice. When he whistled a tune with his lips, the little boys in the township came out from the street corners to see him, so did the birds from their warm nests. Tshupi got along very well with everyone. We crowded around him to listen to his fascinating tales about animals in the forests. Sometimes he related to us movies he claimed to have seen at the Rio Bioscope. He was a few years older than us. On Saturday mornings my mother would often send him to accompany me and my brothers to a fish shop in Dasi to buy masbhanka fish. My mother would then ask him to clean the raw fish and dry it in the sun for our evening meal. In the right mood he was a responsible guy.

I was busy looking at the world with bright eyes. My mother always taught us to be thankful for the little that we had. She bought us black shoes for school and church. We had no shoes for rainy days, but I had a favourite blue and yellow raincoat. It went down my legs to just below my shins. Many days I wore that raincoat in the windiest of weathers and in the brightest sun.

Tshupi's young brother, Sakhiwo (we called him Khiwo), was a different kettle of fish altogether. He liked wandering all about the township alone, not really wanting to be with anybody. No one really knew what dark ideas and missions were brewing in his young head, as he was entirely secretive. But at the same time he could be surprisingly candid in conversation, outright and eager when he wanted to be understood. He was also a great storyteller, highly original and extraordinarily imaginative. Many years later, I would think of Tshupi and his dreaming brother Khiwo as the main inspiration behind all my chaotic writings. I also wanted to talk about hidden truths, to write about a world where nothing germinates and nothing blooms. To write about the hard block of frozen ice that we called our cherished home. I found despair in politics. My eyes wanted to study the dry lakes of the world. I was bound in musical prayers and hearty laughters. I was not interested in bedrooms. What made me real was the sound of the heart beating. I had no premonitions. In my world there was no space for prophecy. For several hours in any day I became like my young friend Khiwo, an island or lake that had been forgotten.

Khiwo was much younger than me, about my young brother Seko's age. His iintsomis (for that's what his fantastic stories were) were all rooted in distant ravines and jungles, populated by flying fairies, scheming ogres and enchanted jackals and wolves. All the creatures that came out of his head were charming in a humorous kind of way. Every creature in his stories could talk, in English or isiXhosa or even Afrikaans. He would imitate the sounds and words made by the wily jackal as he fooled umVolfo with an uncooked meal, "Vrityi vrityi vrityi, umngqusho uvuthiwe! Vrityi vrityi vrityi, ndithi umngqusho uvuthiwe!" Frogs, spiders, stones, rivers, leopards, thikoloshes, giraffes, mirrors, house doors, forests, dying angels and garden walls, they all spoke in a secret language whether they were upset or happy, or flying away from the land of the winds to the big home of the star angel. For Khiwo, all animals in the world had hidden wings. Even plants and flowers could fly sometimes. Anyone could see animals and flowers flying or talking excitedly if they look around carefully in the township.

Khiwo's storytelling gifts were boundless. We would sit next to him and listen to his enchanting voice, his stories completely fascinating us, laughing till our stomachs forced us to go to the outside toilets to pee or shit. Jackals and wolves didn't only wear clothes but put on three-piece suits, ties and sleeping gowns. At times they also wandered about in the forests of the world carrying guns and knives. His stories enacted his curiosity and nightmares about the many faces of the bizarre city that encroached upon our poor lives, making its deathly presence felt around our township, confounding everyone, including our parents, with its fascinating disguises and lies.

I was still a small child when I woke up to face my fears. The spirit of darkness was upon me. It informed me that horses' hooves would come to crush my body. My limbs would be impoverished and all the holes of my heart that were leaking pus or blood would remain without hope, like the poor Hozana traders at Njoli Square street market.

My brother Mbambeleli stood and faced me, one hand on his waist. He was agitated. His chest was heaving noticeably and his eyes looked venomous and huge. "Mxolisi, what are you doing? Have you lost your mind? Why must you always look for a scolding from Mother?" My stubborn silence angered him. I dumped the heavy black bag from my shoulder onto the ground. I continued digging a hole in the black earth that we used as a vegetable garden in our backyard in Madala Street.

I walked into the woods one day and I could not walk out. I walked into a grove with running streams and I heard poetry being recited. In awe I stood and watched insanity grow. I watched children grieve into sunset, driven like slaves into the valley of a bending river. All in a single line, driven from houses with no doors into the bleary silence. A guard stood behind them with a whip and a smile and smoked.

Where I stood, the black forest blinded my eyes and silenced my fears of all the beatings in the world. The forest hid luminous spirits and menacing goblins. One night the Lord of the Forests, referred to by his three million wives as NEXT WORLD, convened an important gathering. Heroes and bandits from all parts of the world were called. The voice of the Lord of the Forests was sad.
"Humans are plotting against us."
"Humans are traitors."
"Let us collect money and light the candles and the fire in the wood."
"Death will snatch the babies."
"The forest will harass the women."
"The old people will denounce their ancestors."
"What about the words men speak?"
"What about their language?"
"The sky will burn the tongues of the living ones!"

Maybe these endless hallucinations were the first clear signs of poetry in my life. I searched for poetry in simple places, in hospitals and in places of overwhelming beauty

22

or sadness. At first I was confused, but after a while I became elated, speechless with a strange madness. I began to notice that the sun is like a far-off planet in the blistering distance, a regal monster with besmirched clothing. I researched the customs of the hobos and the drunken people in the township. I tasted their bitter liquor, and got drunk from umqombothi, the native beer that is brewed in the open, under the terrible sky. During the deep night my solar plexus grew its own enigmatic wings, and my eyes revelled in the sight of formidable kingdoms and magnificent revolutionaries.

One early morning, sitting on a wooden bench outside our local spaza shop, I softly turned up the maskandi sounds of "Lavuth' ibhayi", Saba Mbixane's traditional music show on Umhlobo Wenene FM. In the floating sounds of maskandi I found the green nutritious leaves for the cautious words that sang in my bones. Saba, an exhilarating DJ, was a significant voice. He could explain the inner life and the hard lyrics of maskandi better than anyone. His connection with the music's fluidity and lyrics awoke within me the poems that I so desperately wished to sing.

I went to see a maskandi show in KwaNdokwenza, a despicable and down-beaten hovel of hostels in KwaZakhele, just outside Bhlawa. Ndofanaye (We will die together) Community Hall was built on a huge outfield on the edge of a sharp slope where the brown earth was black in patches and cracked with mud and stones. I entered and sat on a chair broken by the dew, my eyes wet. The maskandis descended onto the stage wearing green dresses and red hats. Some of them were smoking mbheka-phesheya pipes and looking extremely defiant, bright and colourful in appearance like peacocks. Not a single one of the vituperative maskandis on the stage that day was wearing even a sandal on their feet. They all floated upwards, like something was lifting them off the ground to walk on air. Small children in similar attire, carrying long thin sticks like shepherds, followed behind with unfaltering steps, singing and dancing. Bewildered and full of useless questions, I stood and observed the bleary-eyed men and women around me in the hall who wore plenty of sandals on their huge feet. They were the happy people of God from the Zionist church, whose long blue and white robes swept the earth as they walked softly towards the black horizon, dancing to their weeping gods. A heavy stench of human waste drifted inside the packed community hall, invading the eerie sounds of squeaking guitars and choking human voices. I was a happy child that day, the world around me at Ndofanaye a constellation of blue stones, full of colour and magic.

At home I would wake up from a midday or an early morning nap convinced that I had overhead all the conversations that went on during my sleep in our tiny house in Madala. Maybe my subconscious mind was indeed a daytime prowler who slipped out of my sleeping body and sauntered about the mazy streets of Bhlawa disguised as a shadow. It bothered me that no one at home took any notice of my soul's escapades. I would work myself up into a fit trying to convince my parents about the numerous conversations that I had heard in my sleep, as my spirit loomed and wandered about the kitchen or dining room.

"I came into the room just as you were reaching out for your cigarettes on the table Tata. Ma was sitting over there

24

mending a shirt. You were talking about our school fees."
I would blurt out these dramatic revelations to a bored
audience. But no one cared to listen. They had other
significant businesses of the real world to focus their lives
on. But many years later I would meet poets who saw the
world as I did.

5

My grandfather's house was in eZivranda, a small block of zinc houses next to Red Location. Each one had a small veranda overlooking the oldest corrugated iron houses in the world. I rarely talked to my grandfather. Sometimes he would sit on a sofa and talk softly to us. A lonely bird would fly gently in the grey sky to inform us of the coming winter rains. Then the men in eZivranda would all come out in their numbers to fix the leaks in the zinc roofs properly so that the bitter winds of Port Elizabeth would not blow their houses away. The TC White Hall stood a few metres from my grandfather's house. It was a large building, intimidating and tall among the derelict surroundings. Its name honoured a man who none of the eZivranda residents nor I knew anything about. During those days, our people kept their eager questions and their anger at the callousness of the world deep inside the hidden rooms of their hearts.

Quite recently, I found a folder with old photos of my family. I must have brought it from Madala last year after some spring cleaning of my mother's room. Inside there were some old letters including one from my grandfather to my mother and father, dated 24/09/1980, thanking them for a R50 that they gave him during a church trip to Cape Town.

Dear Son and Daughter.
I take this opportunity to apologise for delay in refunding the R50 you helped me with. I fear to go light-pocketed in

such a journey and I'll send it on my return.
The wound is healing but not complete. Your help is
invaluable and from our Heavenly Father through you.
I'll write you on my return. So many things were waiting for
me. I am not through them yet.
God bless you and my grand children.
J.Y. Hliso.

Writing letters to his daughters in the colonial language
was a source of prestige and learning to my grandfather.
His aspiring towards the English was also a means of
survival. Colonialism had taught blacks to deny themselves
their languages and cultures. People of his generation took
pride in the Queen's English which they learnt in school.
Everyone wanted to be an English gentleman or lady. I
think my grandfather felt he had to present the best of
the English world to his children, so that they could follow
after him, and survive, and even prosper in the world. This
was something that he began very early from what my
mother told me.

He was a teacher by profession. He came from Centane in
the Transkei. He experienced the first signs of ancestral
calling when he was still a very young man, but decided to
squash this calling by joining the church, abandoning his
teaching profession and becoming ordained as a church
minister. He married young, a girl from Pietersburg, my
grandmother. She died very young. My mother never knew
her, only her older siblings had experienced her love. So
the young deacon had to raise his family of four alone.
When one of his daughters, Pela, my mother's older
sister, started to chant and dance alone, experiencing an
ecstatic spell, my grandfather was gravely concerned. He

discouraged her with a heavy hand, warning her against any possession by her ancestors.

Many years later I discovered that my grandfather had written a small book of religious sermons called *Wena*. One sprightly day in October, when it had been raining for a week, my mother asked my brothers and myself to open the large card-boxes that had been stored for months in the outbuilding. Inside these card-boxes were piles and piles of a small green book, *Wena*, all packed neatly in careful rows. Mother asked us to hand the books out to our neighbours in Madala.

The book was an isiXhosa book of religious sermons about a foreign god who descended from a heaven in the sky to save the world. I'm not sure whether this book saved him from his African ancestors. We were all pleasantly surprised to read from a book that was written by a living person, somebody we knew. We had always thought that all writers of books were dead people. Deep down I wanted to believe that my grandfather was trying to redeem himself by writing his book in his home language, isiXhosa. But very few of the stubborn people that I knew from my childhood would have agreed with me.

My grandfather wrote his book during his retirement years, in the early 80's. He died in 1984. I inherited his typewriter and I used it for years to write my poems. His obsession with the English world aside, he did his best under trying circumstances. Has his world really changed that much? Aren't we still living in the same old world, except with new gods? Will the next generations condemn us black writers for writing in English? Where do the criticisms end?

One day someone accused me of betrayal for writing my book *Malikhanye*, to my son who passed away, in English. Was that a fair criticism? Where and how do we begin to correct the wrongs? There are so many. And so few of us fight against our oppressors.

6

One day a stranger arrived at our doorstep carrying a black suitcase. It was Aunt Nhoyi, a relative from my father's side who arrived in Bhlawa that day from eRhini, to work as a domestic servant in the kitchens in Summerstrand. Aunt Nhoyi stayed with us for several months. She was a larger than life person who loved the company of her friends and enjoying a good time.

"Mxolisi," she would say, doing the washing or fixing properly the curtains on the wall, "how unkempt and tedious you keep yourself!"

She was so lavish with life, all the time spoiling my young brother, Seko, with fruit juice and all kinds of sweets from town.

Aunt Nhoyi always made sure to divide her time in those days between our small family and her countless friends, who seemed to come from every street corner in the township. Her extravagant nature brought endless havoc to us, putting a heavy strain on the family as it brought into our lives all sorts of ill characters. One of her closest friends was Sis Sphoki, a woman who was notorious for shoplifting in town and stealing wet clothes from the washing lines in the neighbourhood.

"I'll be glad, my husband," my mother pleaded with my father one day, "if you could talk to Nhoyi about the people that she brings into the house. The children are growing up fast. It is not good to them to be exposed to all these bad people who come in and out of the house to see Nhoyi."

Father stood there impassively. When he went out into the dining room to fetch his cigarettes his face grew black outlines on the side as if he was thinking too much. At that moment he seemed to be pulling with all the combined strength of his body at a world that was slowly sinking, gradually falling down into the ground.

Two days later a telegram arrived from eRhini. I was on my knees polishing the stoep when the postman approached with a friendly smile, handing me a slip to sign.
"Don't worry, Mxolisi," said Aunt Nhoyi, who had just come outside into the yard from the house, smiling, "I will sign everything."

From the day of that telegram, life at home took a dramatic turn. The telegram from eRhini was an urgent note from our grandmother, Nontsapho, pleading with our parents to accommodate her son Ndawo during the time he would be in Port Elizabeth to look for work. More bed space had to be found to accommodate him. Aunt Nhoyi continued to sleep in her bed in the children's room. My young brother, Seko, who was about two years old, slept in our parents' bedroom. I and my two older brothers had to sleep on a mattress in the dining room. Bhut' Ndawo used the old couch in the outside cabin as his bed at night. He always seemed so peaceful.

Ndawo had lost his job working at a horse farm in Sevenfountains, just outside Grahamstown. But no sooner had he joined our family than things started to disappear from our house – washing rags, clothes, toothbrushes, clothes pegs, shoe polish, even a steam iron and its ironing board. He would go about the house mumbling to himself.

31

I would arrive at home from school and the house would be filled with the worst drunkards in Madala Street.

One day I arrived at home to find Nontsapho, my grandmother, sitting on a chair on the veranda outside. We later learnt that Nontsapho had taken a train and travelled to Port Elizabeth alone. Later that same afternoon, when my father asked her about her journey and the reason for travelling such a long journey alone at night from Grahamstown, Nontsapho was dead silent. She stopped responding to the world. Her eyes moved languidly and with some effort, eventually fixing their gaze on the chair or at the wall for hours. She never said a word. Her refusal to speak continued the next day. On the third day of Nontsapho's abstinence from the world, my parents called an ambulance. She died at Livingstone Hospital that same week, still not having uttered a word to anyone.

7

The children's room in Madala was always exceptionally crowded with clothes and books. My mother always bought books. It was a reading home, except for my father who just sat in his chair smoking his Van Ryn's cigarettes. At school we competed for the best marks as top students in our classes. Our lives were dominated by school and the strict disciplinarian measures that our father exercised. Along with my two brothers, Mbambeleli and Vusumzi, I grew up detached and protected from the violent world of the white man, free from external persuasion and authoritarian oppression. I was just beginning to write poems. Political unrest had made going to school classes an impossible mission. The black townships were no-go areas.

Mbizweni Square in Bhlawa was always busy with young boys and puberty-charged schoolgirls fooling about, smoking cigarettes, playing loud music, and avoiding the scolding frowns from the adult men alighting from the Algoa busses from work. I would move past the crowds of onlookers and curious bystanders on my way to Mantuntu, our township grocery store. I enjoyed running to the shops on errands for my mother. I must have looked ridiculous running like a demented ghost up Mendi Road on my way to KK Butchery at Mbizweni Square to buy mincemeat or tripe. A young man, probably one of my elder brother Mbambeleli's school friends, would call out, "Hey kwedini, you just look like your father. Where's Mbadz? You must tell him abantwana balahlile (the girls are all out). He must come and join us." I would acknowledge him with a slight nudge of my shoulders, smile back and rush past to the vegetable store Sponono, to buy a 20c plastic bag of potatoes for our family's supper.

At school I was impressed by guys (and sometimes girls) who defiantly stayed away from school without their parents' knowledge. Every morning they woke up and prepared for school like any normal learner but then wandered about all day in town, doing nothing in particular. I remember how one of them, Ngeni, used to bunk school. He would ready himself for school, that is, wash his face, eat breakfast, brush his teeth, put on the school uniform, polish his black shoes, take his school bag, set out for school. But then he would turn back, to re-enter his father's house. First he made sure no one was around to see him. Then he would proceed to climb up the fence, scale up a high wall and jump up to the roof. He stayed up there the whole day long, reclining against the chimney or lying flat on his back, hardly moving. The people inside the house would be thinking the boy is busy at his desk in school, learning to become a model citizen of the world, while on the roof Ngeni would be listening to everything that was happening inside the house, hearing people's deepest secrets.

For many days I sat in my room in Madala facing a whiteboard that I hung on the wall to work on my algebra. Everything came together in numerical figures and variables on the whiteboard. I threw myself into them, staring for hours at complex algebraic equations and finding swift methods to reduce the expressions to their simplest forms. I got so much into algebra that I sometimes forgot to take my meals or go to the toilet. My eyes lit up when something equalled 0 or 1. I thought God hid in the equations or behind the variables, and solving for x meant identifying the holy presence.

I lost weight and my eyes began to water and itch. I ignored this and simply refused to slow down. I quickly became constipated with my tensions. I grew miserable and small. I thought my death was imminent. I sat in my small room in Madala facing a black window and a white wall with no pictures, ruminating about small geometric shapes, calculating the busy life-span of numbers. My flights of algebraic fancy ended abruptly when it came to me, with a sudden and terrible force, that God manipulates the variables. Life's problems would never equal 0 or 1. It was all a waste of time.

I quickly went back to being a pessimist. I wished the fighting in the streets would come to an end and the gunshots fall silent. I wrote a dark poetry of ghoulish men and women with uncertain futures. My freedom came one day from a *Reader's Digest* book, in an article about the Spanish civil war, which concluded with the blue words of a Garcia Lorca poem. This poem pointed to an exit door from my dungeon. Its language of hope and healing burnt to ash all the murdered. I was in higher primary school then, Johnson Marwanqa. It was just before the 1980 school boycotts. I did not partake in any school sport. I despised the school's choir which felt like a soldiers' regiment, firing horrible notes at everyone.

At school we had a green poetry book called *The Oak and the Peach* that was set for our English class. It was in that green book that I read Mafika Gwala's wonderful poem, "One Small Boy Longs for Summer". My heart melted. I felt the warm sun on my back. Even the birds had their voices and they talked to me. One of the first books that I ever bought with my own money was *No More Lullabies*, Mafika Gwala's second poetry collection, published by Ravan Press in 1982.

The singers in the township played sombre music like gods. They drank mischief tea like common people. The African Jazz Pioneers' music sounded to me like the voice of a small hut left alone in a dry field. One woman went there with her heart's strings severed in two. I was enthralled by the throbbing pulse of the horn until a lost capillary of blood was cut. The hard strings broke inside and something else was posted in their place – the earth's wild and unruly sinews tampered by the winds. *The Bull and the Lion* by Ratau Mike Makhalemele and Winston Mankunku Ngozi. The rastaman Eddie Grant who once asked a powerful question in his lyrics, "Do you feel my love? Do you feel it when I walk away?"

Dennis Mpale was another great magician with music. He reinvented jazz, created his tempestuous and buoyant rhythms. We continued for years waiting for the next single from this great jazz-kwaito composer. His delivery and his interpretation, his mastery of the horn were extraordinarily superb. I have yet to hear an artist with such grace in his music, committed to playing the soul's onerous demands. Yet even in his death Dennis Mpale's life and music remained silent and unknown, hidden like dark matter.

8

There was so much that I didn't know. I asked my father about life and got no answer. He was a man of action who didn't think much about the behaviour of animals and humans, or why the sun went up every morning the way that it did, or why so many things including stars, died suddenly, erased from their chaotic lives like they were never born. All these were traumas which gave me many sleepless nights. I was worried about the beggars in the streets and their lives, which brought bewilderment to people. I was fascinated by the settling dust on our furniture at home and the ticking wings of the giant clock on the wall. I wondered at what time the black crows would fly out in the evening. Many of my friends at school believed that words had no power over guns and machines, that technology and science were superior to human conversation. Well, not me: poetry moved out of its prison for me those days.

I often found talking to people in Bhlawa distressing. Some of my friends completely terrified me with their dreams of success. I had no heart for lonely ambitions. From where I stood, nothing was going anywhere. School had not assured me of any future. My parents didn't have enough money. Profound poverty was waiting for me down the short road of my dismal black life. Feeling weighed down by the world, I resorted to words to release the heaviness that I felt in my heart. Without poetry, the empty sockets of my eyes and my sliced hands would have been digested inside the grumbling stomach of the Casspirs. My father was a strict man, intolerant of dissent or indiscipline within the family. Yet from him I learnt to be soft and pliable like a reed. His lessons of love also taught me perseverance. He taught me to stand my ground. I often heard tales of how defiant men, locked inside the grey walls of state hospitals and solemn prisons, were broken down slowly to become soft like the insides of men's eyes.

Mother God had laid out her bare intentions for our community, meticulous plans of countless graves in Veeplaas for the poorest and weakest in our community to bury one another on weekends. Every Saturday the township came alive with mourners' marches and songs. The anguish of funerals was always mixed up with the partying sounds of the jovial taverns where people danced their miserable lives away. "Is that Babsy playing?" came a loud voice from somewhere in a busy tavern. Nobody was ready to answer, and the question was quickly drowned by the general noise of the patrons. I learnt with bitterness about the long agony of the human soul in the songs of Babsy Mlangeni, the blind local music superstar. I liked his pessimism:

Ndiyimfama	I am blind
Ingathi uyandoyika	It appears like you are afraid
Ndiyimfama	I am only a blind fellow
Ndifun' ukuwela umgwaqo	Who wants to cross a road

A few of my teachers were convinced that I was a most capable learner, that I only needed their guidance to avoid a fateful end. But one day my physical science teacher asked me to go with her to the principal's office. I had to answer to all forms of fabricated lies against me, accusations that I was influencing the science class to boycott classes. The principal demanded to know if I was smoking dagga. My parents were summarily called to the school for a meeting with the school principal. My mother sat silently on a chair in front of the principal, Mrs Blydom, listening to the trumped-up charges, stupefied. I was given the choice of taking twenty lashes on my backside or facing immediate expulsion from my school. Vicious strokes on my buttocks were heard in the nearby classrooms, some cutting my back and hands as I tried in vain to ward off the violent whipping from the cane of Mr. Meyer, our Afrikaans language teacher.

I continued to wander about Bhlawa fascinated by our grimy surroundings. I kept a craziness about me, an attitude of mind about the world and its inhabitants that somehow insulated me. The buttons of my collared shirt, that I always wore with delinquent pride at Kama Primary School, were torn off one day by the rough hands of a school bully. We had lots of those, especially from Red Location or eLalini eBomvu, a poor neighbourhood that thrived on disorder. Black townships were ruled by two heavy hands of strict order: the white government which detested black people, and the gilded hands of the tsotsis and small-time hagglers. The time was precisely two o'clock when I rushed inside our house, my white school shirt almost flying off, and threw my school books on the table. I did not understand anything.

9

Growing up in a family like ours with two working parents, we children often had no one to look after us. Our parents did the best they could do, but they could never be present continuously to cater for our needs. As a result my brothers and I often struggled to keep up with the progress of other kids around Bhlawa. Our Bantu Education, poor as it was, was interrupted by the school boycotts, strikes, and police raids of the 1970s and 1980s. Young people like us have sometimes been called a 'lost generation', and they were not wrong to say that. I was lost most of the time. I never quite knew what was expected of me. I never knew how to begin a conversation with the apartheid system which sought to dehumanise me. I grew afraid and became wild. When I stared at a newspaper, I imagined that behind the black letters on the pages there were extravagant voices that were muted in sleep, places where children lived happily, worlds with no angry soldiers or police, where calm and resignation transformed easily into flowers, and wet skies covered the clouds.

I stretched my legs and began my walk to my school, half a kilometre away, carrying my school bag over my shoulders. A boy who always stood at a corner of Mendi Road smoking a zol, greeted me during my walks to school and around my township. I wanted to erase from my memory much that I found intriguing and wildly boisterous about our world in Bhlawa – things, happenings, and people I found too contradictory for my peace of mind. I wanted to make a public demonstration of my love for words. I resented my friends who I felt hadn't yet mastered the art of conversing with the dead, or invisible friends, or flying spirits from other worlds, ancestors who appeared in dreams as bees and other insects. There at Mbizweni square, where groups of boys and girls were partying, I wanted to go onstage and sing my poems for the whole world to listen.

At school my maths teacher taught me to be patient with the world, to act slowly. To look at two or three things with the eye of someone who never rests from looking and thinking. In this way the geometry of the world emerged. A husband leaves his wife and children and elopes with a beautiful twin. The room they enter appears awkward pictured from a camera. The small house is built on a steep hill. To get up to the top you crawl on all fours. A window faces a tired looking structure, a grim cliff, a granite rock. The room has no ceiling. A green chair stands in the middle. The room is hollow like a grave. One angle of the crumbling balustrade stairs appears slanting down from an obtuse plane, like a drowning ship. The other angle moves on with the times, apparently not bothered at all that everyone else shits hard rocks and stones every other night in the communal toilets.

One night the soldiers came to Madala Street brandishing their many weapons. They were coming to mock a defenceless people. We were poor and hungry, afraid of the might of the law, and we had no weapons to defend ourselves. The white soldiers came and cheerfully drove us out of our warm beds into the dark night in the middle of a raid. I was sleeping and dreaming of mystical things when I thought I heard a voice calling to me from a distance, "Mxolisi, come to us. Come, come and join us. Be with us and you won't be a lonely child anymore. We will protect you!" I was still quite young and impressionable. I grew animated and wanted to run away with my new friends whose faces were masked by the blackest tar. The shorter one exchanged quick glances with the one whose well-oiled face glistened under the starlight. I broke free from their hard embrace. I ran for kilometres without end driven by a primordial force towards crowded streets and gesturing faces of the sleeping township. I heard only my mother's warm voice beseeching me to run. All our family's persecution had to come to an end. One drowning in the night, one swift escape from the long arm of the law, the dutiful hands of soldiers and the police, and I would be free forever.

In some ghetto townships around Johannesburg, Cape Town and Port Elizabeth, the older students' boycott was almost total, according to school officials ... 340,000 fail to show up. "Radical disruption of school has already done incalculable harm," state-run Radio South Africa said in a commentary reflecting government views: "Without an intensive and uninterrupted program of education, the country faces a future of exploding unemployment, unmanageable social and economic dislocations and chronic instability. The time had come to act with determination to re-establish a normal environment for black pupils to get the schooling they must have." In Port Elizabeth, long a stronghold of the outlawed African National Congress, most blacks either did not go to work or returned home if they did.

– Los Angeles Times, July 15, 1986

42

"He is not the trouble-maker!"

"Then why is he standing here?" the burly white soldier asked, scratching his elbow and looking at the hidden face behind the loudhailer. Hidden Face was perched up high like a bird in the towering armoured Casspir. I stood just a few metres below, beneath the blistering light of the super-powerful searchlight that Hidden Face and his friends shone on us.

"He can go back to bed. He is too small. We are looking for the comrades. Where is Bhongo?"

"Who is Bhongo, Meneer?"

"Shut up kaffir! You know him."

"You are all under arrest! You burned Mr Majozi's house last night."

That night I saw the soldiers drag Dumi's father by the scruff of the neck and throw him inside the open mouth of a yellow police van – what we called a mellow yellow. Inside the mellow yellow other prisoners were already crouched on the floor like cockroaches, awaiting their sudden end.

My parents sent me to a rural school to escape the school boycotts. This school was in the district of KwaNothemba in Bhofolo. It had hostels for boys and girls, a long desolate field separated the two hostels. Visits between the boys and girls were not allowed. An old man who struggled to see in the dark shuffled his feet through the cold night, guarding the behaviour of the older boys.

I was the dreaming boy who was unafraid of dying. I had not damned God nor despised a single member of his family. I became used to wandering. A steep mountain cut the tenuous dirt road that led to the small town of Bhofolo, keeping our school isolated from the outside world. I had a vision of small and large taxis driving up and down, backward and forward, in unfathomable directions over an endless earth.

Fortunately for me I was used to wandering in streets that were littered with tsotsis. I was familiar with the dark halos of the world and with lost and beguiled souls. At my first sight of heaven on a small koppie littered with ants in KwaNothemba, I stood for a minute outside the long street, at the immovable gate of Lost Paradise, and thought of an escape. The cold wind bit hard like a piercing razor blade inside my flesh. It was Friday 3 a.m. The day had not even started. At the administration building of Lost Paradise I observed sly looking beggars, sitting at an empty table. No one I knew was there. There was a sad looking guy with a black mooring rope and a long whip performing a trapeze act with jugglers, tightrope walkers, gazelles and acrobats. In a quiet corner of the imposing tent there were cold women and thirty frolicking beggars with smelling armpits.

One night, when I was far away at Thubalethu, the rural school in Bhofolo, the young comrades pelted our house in Madala Street with stones. They were demanding that I abandon my studies in Bhofolo and come back to Bhlawa to join the liberation struggle. A note written in blood and plastered with cellotape around a rock was found near a broken window pane. Its message was brief, "uMxolisi makabuyele eBhayi kule veki okanye le ndlu izakutsha." (We will burn down your house if Mxolisi isn't back in PE this weekend).

Fearing the comrades would carry out this threat, father

instructed that I board a bus home the following day. I came back to Port Elizabeth to wander the streets, dodge police bullets, and breathe in teargas along with smoke from burning bodies. Some of my friends were repeating slogans like, "Each one Teach one / One Settler One Bullet / We must kill the Boers / We must murder our enemies like pigs / Pelt or shoot them down like birds." I wondered who were these people that we were being asked to slaughter. It took two years before the schools opened again.

My mother had just borne Seko, my youngest brother. I again had to come back to Port Elizabeth, this time to help with the domestic chores at home. And now that I remember this, I discern a pattern. Many years later, after my ailing father had suffered a massive heart attack, my mother called on me to come back from the University of Transkei, where I was in my final years of study, to look after him. I have always been a helper, the one who consoles everyone.

For his thirty years of hard and loyal service, the insurance company Old Mutual honoured my father with a bright green suit and a matching tie with a silly emblem. That signature emblem on the bright green tie always fascinated me, a golden brown logo which followed an undecipherable spindle like a sleeping viper. It was ominous, intimating wealth and a lust for power. Yet one night my father's green suit saved our lives. Word had gone round that the soldiers were going to raid Madala Street to look for comrades. For an entire week my father would hang his green suit neatly in our sitting room on a nail against the wall every evening, in clear view of everyone.

That week the raids started. At 3a.m. the soldiers came and marched people out of their houses at gunpoint to stand on parade outside in the cold street. As his henchmen started persecuting us inside our house, the captain's eyes fell on the green jacket. He wanted to know its owner. His brother in Pretoria worked for Old Mutual. He talked with my father for a minute, then instructed his troop to march us out. When my two brothers and I were about to be forced into the back of the Casspir for our arrest, the captain issued an instruction to his henchmen to immediately release us. In his eyes my father's suit qualified us to be humans like his brother in Pretoria. That is how unbelievably cruel life was in South Africa under apartheid. Green suits mattered more than people's torments.

10

"Mxolisi, uyaphi?" where are you going? It was my friend Dumi, asking with a sparkle in his eyes. I had a book in my hand and I was in a hurry. I had heard that the Bhlawa Library had been burnt to ashes by the comrades. The book in my hand was already overdue and I didn't want an unnecessary fine.

Dumi had been walking around the township one night when he felt a dominant presence accompanying him.
"Ah! If only I could escape from my body!"
"Ah! If only I could be rescued from my friends!"
Dumi stumbled on forward. He was nearing Ghosts' Village, time was travelling fast. It was ten o'clock and the green houses of the township were closed early. There was disappointment in the cold streets. The spirit that was following him started to cry in a sympathetic voice.
"God is good to all of us."
"God is the King of Kings."
"God is good to all of us."
"God is the King of the road."
And so at that hour, when he was being transported swiftly to the House of Death by a weeping ghost, Dumi was finally saved.

Though I was a very imaginative child, full of ghost hallucinations myself, I could not believe Dumi's story. But I could see that my friend was now a changed man. In one night he had grown to be a solitary preacher of good. His great soul was now divided between a brilliant faraway heaven and our ghostly township. His passionate supplications to heaven for mercy for our piece of hell agitated and tormented me for many many long nights.

One memorable day the South African Police took aim to shoot us in the back for crossing a busy street. I was a young impressionable poet on the way to Korsten Library with a pen in my hand, and Dumi was with me. A mellow yellow police van stopped suddenly right on the highway, at the intersection traffic lights of Commercial Road. Two young white police guys jumped out of the vehicle, and pointed their guns at us. Dumi was highly agitated. He kept muttering something, moving his hands frantically about with jerky movements. One of them shouted, "Waar gaan julle? Staan net daar!" (Where are you off to? Stand right there!) Dumi stopped, pressed me to himself clumsily, muttering curses under his breath. "Remember what I'm telling you Mxolisi, we're going to Rooihell today, no escaping!" It was clear that the two young constables were quite eager to use their guns to kill us on the spot. We did not wait to be told the day of the month. We knew that our lives meant nothing to these two young bored white men in blue uniform.

After that incident Dumi never spoke. He would quietly walk past me in the corridor at school, never acknowledging my presence. I found it painful to talk to him. Other boys in the school began to run after him and throw stones at his back.
"Run, run, run Dumisani! AmaBhulu are going to kill you!" the boys would yell at him. I'd pick up a stick and attack the tough-looking boys thinking nothing about what could happen to me.

"What's this that I'm hearing about you and Dumi?" Mbambeleli would ask me at home. "I've noticed that he doesn't come to visit you anymore. Anything bad happened between you two?"

Mother was furious. She talked a little while with Father. In her hand was a ceramic vase which she placed carefully on a side-table. I leapt over to stand close to the back door.

Mbambeleli rushed in holding a round flask. Water was boiling in the kettle.

"Mxolisi's gone berserk, Father! He talks to himself and makes me nervous. I can't sleep at night for he's muttering and making noises in his sleep."

Mother didn't say anything. She fell back on her chair, her woollen dress starting to tear at the seams. Father went to the door, opened it slightly, and looked outside.

"You know about Giddy's police (the security police unit commanded by Lt. Gideon Nieuwoudt). They came for Dumi's uncle last night. Everyone says he was uPoqo and worked underground for umzabalazo."

When I look back at South Africa thirty and forty years ago, I realize we had been in a civil war. I myself did not have an urge to destroy anything. Instead of being violent to my tormentors I avoided them, trained myself to say and do very little in their presence. I saved all my energy for my writing. Father used to say that a good man walks away when a woman scolds him. He told us to never bend to oppression, and use our physical strength properly. He often told us not to expect good news or good fortune. Our family were not a lucky lot. We never found providence and fortune in the world. We always had to toil damn hard to feed our stomachs.

By the time I was a student in higher primary school, I could see that nothing was sacred about the holy church. Neither the crying baby, the flying dove nor the human soul. I despised the Holy Ghost's geometrical tomb which devastated arithmetic.

At home I played the music of Bob Marley or another disgruntled spirit of the Third World in the radio cassette. An unruly element attracted me to shebeens and plump women in black clothes. Prodigious artists like my friend Shepherd, with their rejected art, music and poetry, found a home without judgement in the raucous rooms of a small tavern in Mtimka Street fondly named Nozililo (Home of Tears) by its patrons. I sang softly with the artists. I wrote down on a piece of paper the lyrics of the drifting songs as I heard them, and put it inside a brown envelope.

11

I was with Ngqayimbana, Dumi and Mkhu at Johnson Marwanqa Higher Primary. Throughout our bleak days there we were never fooled by anyone. We just knew that dead town was not friendly to black children. But there in our township, where there was darkness, light would emerge. Despite all the hardship, deep down, we instinctively knew that our township was like a caring mother.

I wore my khaki school uniform at Johnson Marwanqa like an infantry man, a soldier of books. One freezing morning I had to walk to my school barefoot because my only pair of shoes was in a suitcase left behind in Grahamstown. Comrades were shouting "Liberation before Education", a violent political slogan we sang in school. Many of the young black people in my community were living tumultuous lives of struggle and seething poverty, damnation of both the body and the soul. I was puzzled by the rage of my friends. I did not like the people of dead town, but I did not believe that our problems in Bhlawa would go away by butchering their gullible spirits.

Every other day a police squad would arrive at our school in a mellow yellow to pick up boys belonging to the ESP, the Equal Society Party. The police lieutenant would disturb our classes, interrupt our lessons to address us. "Enough of your nonsense! I know some of you – you are crafty devils! You are members of the ESP. We are going to catch you one by one!" The lieutenant would say this so threateningly and when he raised his long finger to warn or insult us, my heart rose and fell with the motion of his red finger inflamed by the violence of his temper.

One day the young comrades of ESP took a man straight from a bottle store and charged him with murder. At 12 midnight they torched him. The man was once a street general, a commander of Ulutsha Lohlang' Olumnyama, or ULO, a rival political group. The general's victim was a different type of snake, a tsotsi from eMaplangeni, a squatter camp in Bhlawa. The overheated comrades burnt people alive in their crude version of human justice.

"Are you now afraid of the comrades?" an upset student leaning over a broken desk asked me. "They burnt a house in my street last night," I answered back. Some of my classmates nodded in silence. I wanted to ask my friends a question but quickly decided against it. I had now experienced the ways of the police, who were eager to pulp us to a fine mess. I had staggered and winced from a blinding pain but remained on my feet, groggy and weak, hardly conscious. It struck me that the police, especially the sadistic Lieutenant Nieuwoudt, always saw their encounters with black students as another opportunity to torment their fellow humans. I admired the ESP for challenging the system for cruelly mocking us, but I did not want to join their atrocities.

Only five years plus one, then I would be completely out of the school system, out of the stiff control of teachers and principals. Not that I hated school, but always felt a deep need to talk for myself, to even speak back and to express myself fully. And our schools in the townships were not allowing any of that. Anything or anyone that was deemed to be too provocative, too challenging to the normal order of the functioning and governance of the schools, was swiftly disciplined and expelled. I struggled to breathe inside the school's buildings. I was not like the other kids. I was sensitive in my soul and too conscious of the enfolding world around me. The hands of the clock were all pointing sideways. They showed a time that was crooked and bent, beaten all the way down to the deep ends of the earth. I could not cope. I had no friends. Nobody seemed bothered that the rainbow in the sky had lost some of its fierce splendour.

These days I look deep into the eyes of white people for any signs of guilt for the sins that apartheid committed in their name. I find nothing there. It is like no atrocities were ever done against the black people of South Africa. White people must begin to live with more modesty, with the actuality of being white Africans in an African country. They have yet to accept the reality of black people on their doorstep who are not just looking for a job from the master and the madam.

12

I tried to smoke cigarettes when I was seventeen years old, but my lungs choked from the heavy Lexington cigarettes inhaled too deeply. I was coughing and drowning. Someone was pounding hard on my back. Tears rolled down my eyes. A girl's voice suggested I go upstairs. For twenty minutes their conversations stopped while I listened to death breathing slowly on my back, making remarks:

"I believe you are going down now."

"Don't cry. They drink coffee in heaven."

"All your problems about your parents and about not being understood, Mxolisi, are things of the past. You are dying now."

I slipped into a disturbing coma. In my coma I walked into a room where two fellows stood waiting for me.

"We were waiting for you."

"We want to speak to you."

"You have become mad."

"We can only restore what has been missing."

"We can fix the days that were not accounted for."

I got up, finished biting my nails, and regarded the two spirits with a startled eye. I could talk freely again. Then I walked off into the spacious building. The whole of the empty building was whitewashed with a thousand birds superimposed like animated shadows along its high walls. A woman called Green Cat started singing a song in a voice that must have been two centuries old. I wondered if the manifestation of her passionate voice could be a sign of something ominous; a thousand lives lost in mysterious circumstances.

After I had complained for weeks about my throbbing headache, my mother took me to see a doctor at Livingstone Hospital. My headache seemed to come from a nerve in my lower left jaw, a decayed molar tooth. But instead of occupying itself with the spoiled tooth, the sharp pain scurried like a toddler running wildly at a playground, along the entire left side of my face, rounding my forehead, finally coming to rest below my crown at the back of my head, just behind my right ear. The headache was a meticulous enemy of my forehead, an invisible but strong-willed alien bombarding my skull bone.

The doctor told me to remove my school shoes and walk barefoot on a rotating machine that kept emitting eerie sounds. I was then asked to fit my head into a hanging dome. Wires with green and yellow plastic ends were attached on my bare chest, and I had to lie still and look up into the dark orifices of a protruding object that was extended towards my head. After I'd been about fifteen minutes crouched and bundled like this, the doctor lifted my right thumb, studied it carefully, touched the palms and then the fingers of both of my hands like he was feeling for something. I waited for him to say something, to tell me that something in my body had gone terribly wrong, perhaps a dreadful African spirit had invaded my thumb bone and my skull. I imagined surgeons and anaesthetists wielding scalpels and steaming needles scavenging my body and cutting away my two hands and my legs just below my knees.

The room at Livingstone Hospital felt weird and exceedingly cold, as if we – the doctor with a lisp, my mother who stood or sat in a chair nearby, the ill looking nurse, and myself – were all trapped inside a big frozen balloon made of helium. "Do you feel anything at all in your hands?" the doctor asked, looking at me sideways while reaching for a metallic object that I suspected he was going to use on me. The nurse moved forward towards the hanging dome, adjusted something on its side, moved it to a better angle to face a huge beam that radiated from lights fitted up above, a little bit askew. I began to feel dizzy, my head swirled to one side of the room, then immediately spun to the opposite direction. "Can you hear me?" the doctor had to repeat three times before I could hear what he was saying. All I could discern as I lay inside the big machine, my eyes transfixed on the two dark orifices, chained to a swirling table, were the quacky doctor's two lips opening and closing in quick successive movements, not emitting any human sound at all.

After a time that felt like the long hours it takes for a dead human to reach eternity, I was asked to lie down on one side of the examination table. With every passing minute the nurse began to look more like a bear. He confessed loudly that he was going to take my life. At least that is what I thought he was saying. My mother, seeing me ready to bolt out of the dreadful building, said "Mxolisi, nurse wants to take your pulse. Lie down on the bed." The doctor had retired into a small corner of the room that I took to be his office, and was now sitting like a praying mantis on a swivel chair behind a long table. The pale nurse, whose name I later learnt was Zungandoyiki, (loosely translated as "I scare no one" or "Don't run away"), wrote something on a pink pad on the table. The doctor sat on his dry chair studying the notes in front of him. After a minute he stood up, as if worn down by life, and asked my mother if she could bring me to the hospital for a second examination the following month, which was May, on a Thursday, my father's birthday.

Children like us were born daily in the street, at the daybreak of funerals like pretty dark birds with wet wings, harbouring feelings of guilt, blind misgivings. They were fated to die alone at the drop of a hat on a lonely day, perhaps a Wednesday or some ordinary summer's evening, blinking at the stars. Yet their suffering was complete. Their solitude surprised everybody, including their parents. In Bhlawa it was better to die alone in the sea, like my friend Ngqayimbana.

Ngqayimbana had died very young, only sixteen years old. Nobody ever told me the cause of his death. At his funeral a preacher mentioned death by drowning, but Ngqayimbana hated the sea. He sometimes joined us on our morning jogs to Bhlawa beach. One day he was there, busy laughing and joking with everybody. The next day, he was dead.

Apparently he had woken up one morning and dressed in his khaki school uniform like he was going to school. But then he changed direction on the way to school and crossed the railway bridge at Mpelazwe, walked past the industrial shops of Deal Party and Carbon Black, and headed straight for the deserted beach. Then he walked into the sea and died by drowning.

In the agony of his funeral at Veeplaas I realized that the

57

only thing that oppressed people do well together is to sing. Other than that, everything is done in loneliness - suicide, rape, murder, death, even love. Things that the old men and women in our township, after much suffering, had understood as private.

13

Some days in Bhlawa were days for suicides and murders. I wondered why deaths often visited us on Sundays. Nothing was ever specific except the suffering. Years later I became a deliberate drinker at Bra Ncesh's tavern in Gqamlana, remonstrating every night with the devil. Life was too short, and drinking alcohol brightened up the days. The poetry I came to live dwelt in poor houses with no pictures hanging on the walls, no tall arched windows. I drank my beer wrested from the world of the crucifix. In Gqamlana someone had locked a dog inside its kennel.

I knew nothing about the cries of children who woke up one day robbed of their lives. Nothing in the world would console my heart except the hard pressure of another tortured being, pain from a kindred heart. Small coffins had to be built very quickly by sorrowful men to bury the tiny bodies in Veeplaas. The graveyard was a huge and desolate field where ghosts and ageless spirits gathered daily to torture the township. It was where I first observed the ceremony of the burial of dead children, schoolkids shot down by the violence of Casspirs and state machinery.

On that Saturday morning my father called out to us, "Come now makwedini, masiwakeni, let us take a walk," calling me and my two brothers for a stroll around the township. It was during that leisurely walk that I saw the black spectacle of that burial. A dark mood hovered above like a predatory animal. The slow events of the ceremony unfolded for a brief second before my eyes as my father ordered us to quickly walk past the roads that led from the cemetery. The burial of the schoolchildren left a permanent and disturbing scar inside me, an image of the commotions and the dying angels.

Everything that could have gone wrong in our lives had indeed gone wrong. The swimming pool at Phendla Street had its waters drained out. Rio Bioscope had perished in smoke. An accident on the road had torn the black curtains of the bioscope down, torn the enchantment of the children apart, and broke from inside the church bells the soul's clamorous anthems. Drunk parties clashed at the corner. Door-to-door visits were performed for the city's elections. A spaza shop opposite our house in Madala Street was burnt down. In the cold street the bandit shoe of the night watchman remained open, confronting the days, contemplating the bolting silence.

Everywhere I went I heard rhythms, and I saw sounds and mystified lyrics. I wanted to breathe under the horrific waves and see things clearly, but there was dust in the air, putrefied animals and insects with brown exoskeletons. There is nothing as defiant as the blue sounds of the township, melodies that march eerily towards my veins. At night I wanted to take a leaf from the melodious wind and step outside into the streets of Bhlawa and sing with the night's alley. To sing of everything that agitated my soul, everything that angles gloriously upward as it empties itself of freedom.

I go to the old church in Aggrey to sing with a young choir, but I am not a singer. My voice croaks like the busy entrails of a dying man. All I want is peace for myself, a sundial's calm in the lecherous wind, comfort for my croaking chest and the burning wings of my soul. Just a few metres away from the old church is eThembeni, the home of the blind of our township, where they sit making reed baskets and chairs, away from the mischievous antics of the sighted. I don't remember much about the house of the blind. My father often talked about the tricks of the eyes that see no further than the human heart.

There was an isolated building in my childhood that never failed to attract my curiosity. I would walk past its high gates that always appeared to me to be hiding an evil cult. I faced the luminous green doors of the building with human wings. There would be nobody in sight. The owners, probably an evil man and woman, recused themselves from the humiliation of the world. It was only many years later that I learnt the true nature of the building. It was the KwaDonki Church of Mendi. But why was there no outward sign on the gates or on the whitewashed walls to reassure us township dwellers of the church's heavenly missions? This was something that never ceased to irritate my curious mind.

In the streets of the unfriendly town of white men, gifts and wreaths were laid out even for the horses that Boer men had ridden out to war. No grief or tributes for the black men and women who were murdered by the police and soldiers in Boipatong and in Langa. I was walking alone in a dead end street when I heard the town weeping. I was foaming at the mouth. A silvery spittle formed a tiny scab just below my left knee. I had no ambitions to follow the party of revellers or to join them in their secret meetings. I saw a flying animal land in a dry place inside a giant bowl. One day the giver of life arrived and opened the bowl to free the spirit of the bird. I noticed a new business in the township, complete with new creatures and plastic malls. We were forbidden to touch the wistful curtains of the shops which – our people were convinced – hid new spells of magic for our destruction. One man met his fate climbing a wall. A woman rubbed the nose of a stray dog and fell from the white stairs. Suicide struck the face of time. The boy carrying a bazooka wrote on a wall: "What saved Jesus's soul those many years ago were the two bad men hanging beside him." The whole town that had been spilling blood in the long night was suddenly on its hind legs, ready to sprint.

On the road to the local tavern I saw foreign men and heard sad pipers' lyrics. In the streets there were children who stared at the lofted moon, drunk and resentful. There were skies where every glint of the sun buried a mole or a wounded child. Every street corner had a black house, a corrupted yard and long gardens that reeked of perfumed winds and cheapened money. The landscape of the place was dead or drunk like its flamingos, burdened by the face of the cadaver. After an hour of being fascinated by the strange surroundings, my trust in people suddenly grew small. I drank tea leaves with a teaspoon of brown sugar. I remained defiant like any distraught man, surprisingly tired and deeply torn inside.

14

Many years later Phedi Tlhobolo, an affable poet from Pretoria, told me that three features always distinguished any black township: the police station, the beerhall or tavern, and the cemetery. We were driving down a tired looking street in Grahamstown in Robert's VW Beetle.

"You see how big the police station is compared to the houses! Once you're inside you can't sneak out."

Yes, at the corner of an indistinct street that was slowly disappearing in the foggy rain, there slowly emerged into my view the splendid building of the Grahamstown police station.

"Were you ever locked in a cell?" Phedi asked. "There's often very little to do while you're there but to sit and wait. Wait for no one. For nobody that you might know will ever be allowed inside. So you sit and wait. You count your breaths. There's often no air to breathe inside a holding cell, although prisons and police stations are always so massive with high windows."

From Phedi I learnt that the first feature that dominates a township is the solid wall of the police station building. It is a work of great charm and longing, an engineer's masterpiece. Its great wall has floodlights shining at night, sometimes even during the day. The existence of bright lights in a police station is understandable. Standing inside one of its huge offices and looking outside produces a calming effect mixed with a sense of wonder. After a few moments like this, experiencing the anaesthetic effect of the police and the station, I've heard that the gazer is overcome by a sudden and urgent need to join the police force. Something like this must have happened to the askaris and impimpis, they who were at first committed comrades during the freedom struggle, but later changed course to join the police. Probably it was the very first time in their miserable lives that they saw the township from the vantage point of a police station. Quite obviously the askaris and impimpis after capture had also become quite disorientated, had their brains rewired, disorganized all over by severe beatings, and relented to the magnetic pull of the force.

The big station always stands there right at the starting point of the township, before the building of the first row of broken houses commences. A sad siren is sounded from the captain's office, and then the impatient builders can start to mix the mortar and erect the first downtrodden house. A police station is an important building in any community, the first reminder to blacks that they are nothing in the world. A reminder that the world will be there after they are gone, buried in their graves in Veeplaas.

Dumi told me that a police squad came to his home one night and knocked down two doors, broke four windows. He went down to the police station to lay a complaint. The big police chief told him that the police were only doing their job, sniffing and sniffing around the poor neighbourhoods where blacks live, like belching whores, looking for fleeing criminals.

Stopping crime in Bhlawa is like fighting cockroaches in a dirty kitchen. They go all over. A million of them can colonize one small place. A cockroach breaks into the house to retrieve something. The house owner is lucky this time, he catches it, then calls the law enforcers immediately. The bored police unit comes eventually, studies the situation, asks the house owner what business he's doing in his house. This surprises the house owner who doesn't really know how to answer. Then the policeman decides right there that no crime was committed. The Captain reassures the house owner with his baritone voice. "Be happy you're safe. You're one of the lucky few. You managed to stop the cockroach before anything serious happened. Make sure you're on Facebook to alert your friends, if not, use your WhatsApp."

The Captain writes down the name and street address of the cockroach. The cockroach has one eye on his face. The other eye was stolen by a cockroach at Dora Nginza Hospital. But this one is lucky to be alive. His ancestors were with him. The house owner and the Captain of the law are tired of his shit. They release him into the kitchen. Free cockroaches roam in a democratic country with daggers in their eyes.

.

The police will never stop spitting and pissing on black faces. You wonder how come the majority of them are themselves black. Black people are expected to love the police deep down, die for them. The police see blacks as criminals. Something in how the police force trains its young recruits teaches them that way. So they sniff and sniff like long-faced dogs around the black neighbourhoods to fish out the bad guys. The richest thieves have moved away, and now stay in the pristine suburbs where the sun melts their hearts. Yes, there is always more for the police in their world of death than buildings and dogs.

An extension of the police station, you could say part of it, is the prison. In my grim thirties I visited Mzwandile Matiwana in St. Albans prison, and brought him a book and old newspapers to read. None of Mzwandile's relatives had ever bothered to go and see him. The day was raining hard. The prison had high walls. It was built at the outskirts of Port Elizabeth town centre, along Old Cape Road, a long road that bellies its way through the entrails of the city, seemingly originating from deep underground. The road, now disguised as the N2, scampers over the midsection of PE, over its highways and subways until it reached Greenbushes, where it pauses for just a little while, observing the prisoners, before hurrying quickly out of the city towards Humansdorp and Knysna, on its way to the Western Cape.

A wide door opened. I was led together with about twelve other fellows who were also visitors, into a large room that looked like a hospital foyer. Idle chairs were pushed all around against its high white walls. This room opened out to another much bigger room with a large table and a round counter. "Going to the waiting room?" a man with a slouched shoulder asked, clapping his hands loudly, closing the black file he was carrying, and replacing it on the shelf. Behind the counter sat two ladies, one eating a banana, the other one attending to her polished nails. Five or eight minutes later, after the guard with a loose shirt had taken our names, addresses, cell phones, keys and ID papers, he led us down the dark passage to a side room with a huge steel door on which three keys dangled. We were all asked to sit down and wait. A minute or two later the door to our right was suddenly pushed open by the warder with the slouched shoulder. And in walked the condemned men, Mzwandile in front of them.

That day Mzwandile passed over to me a letter in a small blue envelope. "This letter is for Sis' Lulu. Please Mxolisi give it to her the next time you see her." My home address was written in neat handwriting on the envelope. Mzwandile told me that he had been desperately saving money for the stamp to post the letter. Prison life was hard. The guards were always looking for bribes from the inmates.

I forgot to give Mzwandile's letter to Lulu. Many years later I stumbled on it by chance inside a cupboard stuffed with old newspapers and books. It had been drowned there in a storage box away from the world for more than fifteen years. Mzwandile had long died, having become a poor and broken homeless man who lived under a bridge. He was afflicted with AIDS and had been on the run from the police. We had been at loggerheads for some time. He did not trust me any more.

The second feature in every black township, Phedi told me, is the beer hall or tavern. There you find blacks experiencing insane merriment, jostling against each other inside the tiny space, drinking a poisonous concoction named hlukuhla, engaging in physical indiscretions in the violent toilets. Blacks emerge from the beer halls, their faces covered with white shit, hair that grew from deep inside their veins, through their skin pores and down their faces and foreheads, dirtying their toadlike nostrils to cover their entire faces like blankets. No, they were never drunk when they were drunk. They sought drunkenness and never found it.

One night I followed a lovely girl with a dimple and a tiny waist like a dolphin. Her name, which flew down to earth from a star with long wandering eyes, was Cikizwa. She came one day and lived in a house next to us with her older sister, Thabisa, who was training to be a nurse at Dora Nginza Hospital. Her parents were in Qombolo in Centane, far deep in the rural Transkei. She had a genuine elegance about her with deep melancholy eyes that came to life every time she smiled. I caught her once outside the spaza shop twinkling those very same eyes, smiling at me, her softened cheekbones making her look so much younger. I was with my friend, Ngqayimbana. I spoke to her and she invited me to her house the following Sunday.

Vanquished by love, I set off to Cikizwa's house to promise her everything under the sun. Her sister Thabisa took one look at me and decided my intentions were not pure.

"You say you want to ask Cikizwa about a textbook? Is she now a school principal?

"No Sisi," I admitted, embarrassed by her questions, "this is a library copy for all the students in class. Today it was my turn to use this textbook. Cikizwa was still busy with it in class and asked me to come and fetch it from her after school."

"Cikizwa is writing a maths test tomorrow. This is a bad time to visit her. But I will call her for you." She turned halfway around and left the room. The air in the house was damp as if it had been raining a tropical storm inside the kitchen. I stood for a minute or two in the kitchen leaning against the sideboard. The small house was nicely furnished with a beautiful brown leather sofa and a big Defy stove and microwave oven in the kitchen.

Cikizwa's father was a police sergeant. It was common knowledge that his adulterous life with women followed him. He was notorious for pulling out a gun and threatening to kill the lovers and husbands of the women he cheated with. That day in Sis' Thabisa's house I wasn't aware that Sergeant Mbanga had come to visit his two daughters. He was there inside the house, probably skulking in one of the rooms on hearing my weak excuse for wanting to see his daughter. Instead of Cikizwa, out from the bedroom came the huge frame of the sergeant with his 9mm pistol.

"Heyi kwedini, ufuna ntoni? (Hey kid, what do you want?) I will kill you if I ever see you again in this house! I will put a bullet in your testicles, masende akho!"

Cikizwa did not show the slightest sign of grief. Her father's temper served only to amuse her.

My punishment for daring to love a sergeant's daughter brought me endless nightmares. I wanted to run away from Bhlawa immediately, go and stay in another township where Sergeant Mbanga wouldn't find me. In fact, one evening I told my three friends, Dumi, Ngqayimbana and Mkhu about my dream of escaping death. This was all so farcical. Everyone stood right there before me on the bent road that crosses Madala Street from Dasi and wished me good tidings and a warm farewell with a heavy shrug of their shoulders. I don't know how long I stood there under a dim streetlight that night to count fading stars in the night sky, half immersed in exaggerated fury, realizing the entire earth had gone dead.

15

I went down the corner street to the same house where I think I was conceived, when my spirit body changed to the body of a human. I was convinced I would meet Philile the blacksmith there. I had a black stone in my hand. In the house lay the silent body of death. I had a premonition of a horrible death with a bullet lodged in my spinal column, and being reduced to a bed at home for the rest of my life. I wanted to be closer to death quickly so that my punishment, when it happened, wouldn't be too heavy to bear in my soul.

It always seemed to me that people transmitted their fears in the clothes they wore, the black or brown shoes on their feet, the red and blue blazers that covered their bodies. The stranger that I met in the house walked around with a strange silence, wearing a green hat, always smiling. He called out, now and again, in a hoarse voice, "Here, here", pointing to a row of lighted steps running to a side room, his eyebrows raised. His red lips were rapidly becoming dry because of his haste to speak everything at once, and he softly drawled again in a hoarse voice, "Can you see what is happening here, and what is written up there? Is it an A or a B?"

Soon after my arrival a dog greeted me on the doorway, a fierce creature with one tiny eye. It leapt forward and started to quarrel with my shoes, growling and roaring like all dogs do to impress their owners. The man struck himself once, then twice, against the shin with the blunt end of a knife. His wife, who was sitting close to the stove warming herself, interfered immediately, "I told you, you must learn!"

After this, everything went quiet throughout the house: the chattering of the mice in the sideboard, the wobbling of a metallic knob on the stove, the dying years which had come down to settle comfortably inside the vestibules of the kitchen sink and the washing machine. They all stood defiantly in the middle of a tiny passage leading to the bedroom, bowing down heavily to the ground, forgiving the man and his innocent wife their obstinacy. The man softly crossed himself, hanging his shameful head closer to the floor. He banged something that was hidden in his left hand against the side table. He tasted the bloody fruit on the raised wooden table in the kitchen. The sun began to set on his face. Everything began to happen so quickly. "Tell me about yourself young man," said the man. "You're such a delicate boy," the wife added slowly. "You must have run very fast to get here." For a moment nothing was spoken by the strange couple. From outside the windows of the house I could see the township was readying itself to sleep.

Later on, the man, who had carried himself with so much self-pity, began to tell me his story. With his ugly face and a tiny voice like a squirrel, I could see he was a greedy man from the land of great lies. He told me he was a ward councillor, a member of the glorious political party that won our people freedom. The chairs in his house were cold as ice. An albatross hovered above his house like a virus ready to strike. There was a new bed in his bedroom. Old furniture had been quickly removed from his living room and thrown out into the street. Expensive curtains with bright decorations were now covering the aluminium windows. Only a few stubborn details of a previous life of poverty remained inside the small house. Pots and clothes reeked with the smell of cadavers and overgrown pink seeds. The side valley where the house stood was always burning.

I am looking for something. What, I don't know. Something that will please or comfort me. A tree. The universe. A dog on a leash. Confusions, straying questions, come into my mind: "You say you can you can you can you can you can you can you can you can you can you can ... and when you are done and your turn comes to say who you really are, you can't. What does this mean? What animal form are you? What is the one thing about the galaxies? How does the hungry Alsatian bitch take careful care of her children? Do the centuries say anything to you? Are you trapped inside yourself in a heartless place, dying? You cannot and you can. You can and you cannot. Your universe." In the streets today the dances of amaZiyoni lighten up my spirits. What comes at first are the primitive sounds of an animal spirit or a hyena that laughs at me harshly.

In a long forgotten room a shebeen queen says breathlessly "You're a poet of a lost language." It is true, I am a surrealist with black words, a hard exilic follower of extinguished stars. A dark pact like a haemorrhaging blood clot forms inside my head where there is a blank hole and emptiness. Last night, in a house in a street where there was no wind, my tired wings clipped by the gruesome face of Christmas, I heard a familiar voice in the trembling night. I came to in a corner of a room, next to a brazier that emitted a wild fire. My drowsy eyes were fixed on a motionless Christ-like figure, ignored or unseen by the voices which knocked loudly on the house doors with their hard fists and shouts of mockery. An old woman with moist eyes was lying on a bed groaning. "Take her to the big hospital near the Grand Parade," a man with a cheek smeared with soot shouted to the guests who sat at the table. Nobody moved or said anything.

I dozed off for a minute in my corner but was soon awoken from my torrid sleep by the sound of Makhulu who was sitting on a stool in the kitchen knitting a jersey, hiding behind a large solid vase. In the other corner sat a man who was half-man and half-mule. His bad smell attracted cockroaches and bedbugs to come out from cracks in the walls, from old clothes stuffed under the bed. These nosy creatures now ventured boldly forward to find themselves a new home inside Donkeyman's shoes and clothes.

Throughout the shebeen were voices and other muffled sounds and inebriated shadows in the hallways. The mistress of the house walked in from an outside room wearing a flimsy gown and slippers. She announced the arrival of more guests, a group of men in suits and their women partners and girlfriends who alighted from a convoy of sedans and SUVs. This new group quickly made their way to a secluded room where braai meat and drinks were served to them by the hostess. The shebeen's rotting smell remained unchanged. Homeless children in the street looked for shelter under the wings of sleeping birds.

At midnight I turned a black eye to affirmation. I chose the moonlight on the skyline of Bhlawa over the sun, the sunlight of death over the stones of eternity. I became silent with no conscious effort. Silence and poetry were my weapons, my bullets and my stones. Life came to me in a small black bottle like caustic wine and vinegar. It felt like suicide. I lost myself in distances and in waiting, in the sad and harrowing habits of life. I lost myself in simple rituals and in people's shadows, in the crooked nipples of funerals. I needed to tie myself intimately to someone, an accomplice in my inconsolable murder. I remembered to hide certain facts about the world. How the earth is celebrated and cheated. How disinterested matter disintegrates, how the sparrows in the township fly. I was grieving for a gifted friend, a poet who chose madness and crime along with the heart's music.

When I looked up at the sky in Bhlawa I saw a finite river that spiralled in cycles like the twelve months of the year. I dreamt white dreams. I saw amagqwirha. The township transformed itself into an effigy of stones. A silent river fell from the sky. People welcomed hate and disengaged the freedom of their spirits. I read books intensely. I waited for truth to reveal itself in the grinding hooves of bulls, in earth's mad erosions and in the chanting hymns of crocodiles. I tremored in my soul. I discovered the horrible magic of life. I was born to live and to die that way, never free from earth's despairs and the desperate sorrows of rivers.

16

My family belonged to the working class. At home we required very little. My mother baked bread in the oven. We broke the walls for the sun to enter the house in the evening, ate our bread and drank our water. Death walked all around us quickly like running angels. I had thought out my task for my life's infirmity. I had figured out the stars. Some of my thoughts disappeared in the plague, flooded out like the sea. They gathered themselves in Red Location, huddled inside a devious building for the dying that the locals named TB Huis. Death carried a spade and dragged its nameless corpses to the graves. The township had no sewage system or electricity. A communal bucket system was used and the place was distinguished by its foul smell. The crown birds of Red Location bade me farewell.

I took little things simply in my hand, not talking to or eulogizing anyone. I went to a poor street where a boy asked me about my future. I met a generation of boys and girls who specialized in various calamities. They wanted me to join them in their heedless games. A dirty horse laughed at me from the border of its insanity. My father, who was planting seedlings in the garden, was outraged. He knew all the skeletons in the cupboards of the workers' party who were marching in the streets that day, demanding decent jobs from the bosses. A dog barked next to the spaza shop in Madala Street, revoking its future. Chaos played out in the corner of a small room in Centenary Hall. They were registering the name of a beggar who had asked them, "What for?" The president of fools was going to talk to the nation that evening. Nine monsters had murdered Bhlawa's children. Bhlawa was burning with impatience.

I had run out of patience with the saga of Bhlawa's torment. In the dead town of capitalists with the rich sea and the poor harbour there were long boats with forgotten oars. The waterfront was bleak. Dead fish and harpooned crabs were strewn like gutted planets on the shore. My poor brothers said I was a drunk. My friends thought I smoked hashish too much. I admitted to every scandal. Where the byways and high roads ended, rich folks had got themselves entangled with the beggars. Their lives were impossible without each other. A tree without morals grew up and rose towards God's heaven in the clouds. The beggars were building the savage town of God's wanton universe with their hands.

I went to an old church building to a meeting for poets to air their grievances with the Department of Arts and Culture in our city. I was invited by a former colleague who phoned me on my cell, a despicable poet who carried dirty spells of magic. The big fellow reassured me with his clever words that had been dunked in a murky syrup. I spent my airtime explaining the coordinates of being, the simple matter of being a citizen of my country with every human right.

In the meeting my DAC friend introduced me as a conservative poet who he'd had to kneel before in order to get me to attend the meeting. The man was leering like a wild horse. The provocateurs insisted that I had to entertain the crowds and sing to them. I told them that I was not a singer but a poet who confronts the sea and writes in defiance of stones. The dark church was suddenly filled with the songs of dead men and crippled women. The whole building was black with the strife of a decaying rainbow. They hated my poetry and demanded from me words that would make the nation smile. Vicious poets lambasted me with accusations, lies, and treachery. I was amazed by this venomous hate between brother and brother, between sisters and brothers. They threw a human skull in my direction, burning stones, cascading waterfalls and bleating sheep. They told me that poets were supposed to be entertainers. What rubbish! Ask dogs what kind of animals they are, and they will readily tell you, "We are dogs." I hid in the irritable century and went on singing my poetry to begrudging stones.

On that grisly night, confronting state officials who only wanted to see soothing performance poets, I knew that I was never going to belong in that godforsaken space of treason. The poets who had gathered in a corner of the sinful house had swallowed the dead town's tombs and released a pneumatic gas that was poisoning the children. They told the drunk mayor "The women are marching in the streets. We are happy to see the women marching in the streets!" They were a noise on the tiny stage, a boisterous anger in my ears!

The officials were determined to push forward with their treasonous agenda. Deep down I prayed that the earth would kill them instantly. Their sleek tongues sought to lie to everyone. And that night there were others present, old men and women who claimed that they were royal members of an indigenous kingdom. These comical monarchs also wanted the poets to suffer. They demanded to hear only complicated recitals and other songs of worship. But why must poets entertain anyone? The artist does not sing for love. He is not an altar boy. Suffering poets never consoled me, nor did I expect them to. They sang to me their dirges and mourning songs. Only the mad state officials believed in lovers' songs. Poetry embodied my disasters. It contained death. Graves and cemeteries opened in the souls of hobos when poets sang. The veins of the tom-toms in a devastated village in the Eastern Cape scattered severed human veils. Poems floated above rivers like the songs of the dead, lyrical and shattering in their music, so that the dove of Medusa swung high like a star at night, splintering the universe into numerous galaxies.

A miserly poet walked up to the stage to receive R60. He was either a man or a beast with ten hooves. The drunk mayor stood in the crowd inside the hall smoking ganja. He got up on a plastic chair and swore at the universe, including the dismal poet on the stage. I saw for the very first time in my life a poet about to be executed in public. Bra Skheps, a poet from the days of COSAW, was the condemned man, looking very ill.

I kept hearing confusing words, "The poets are free! The dead men are running. Their dry words mean nothing. Their women have broken the spell of the mirrors. The black slaves are free!" I was looking for a clue from the ritual songs and unbroken traditions of our ancestors. There were now a thousand people demanding to go to the middle of the dusty church in order to see Bra Skheps condemned by the clergy, to maybe shake his hand as he passed them escorted by big bodyguards on the way to his execution. Hungry people from the township were crouched in the back rows of the building, wishing they had not been born or were still living in the third century. They put the name of Bra Skheps on top of the blacklist and showered him with invective and insults in the place of flowers. I followed his shadow to a side row of the glaring church and told him that no child must weep again. Emboldened by my kind words he went onstage and recited the revolutionary lines of old poets. Then everything in the church died down quietly.

17

The minister of the church, including the one-eyed leader of ESP, who was chairing the meeting, shouted to the conspirators to stop. The bleached wall of the building kept the secrets of the fiends, the murderous intents of the party. All around there were devils wearing pink shoes. I saw a wandering spinster who was cutting her clean nails hour after hour in teary anguish. Her huge stench of birthing the entire township filled up the joyous hall. The township was in mourning. The people were now ready to torch another innocent soul. Strange spirits were skinning their violent hands. Concubines were murdering the mothers of the township. The homeless lepers counted the countless leeches that invaded the black sores of their thighs.

Outside the Rio Bioscope a group of boys and girls play a game of cards and marbles. Next to them a bigger group of street urchins survey the surroundings and studies the shop of the Somali trader. I walk past them and smell their anger. Even the wind in this place is flabbergasted by the boys' destructiveness. They loiter by the fence, intent on burning down the Somali shopkeepers along with the whole street. For some time I stand by the roadside thinking the whole world is coming to an end. One of the girls in a tattered shawl makes an impassioned sound with her cleft lip, her gentle face obliging me to leave the place immediately.

Bhlawa feels like a crazy ghost this morning. The smell of

urine and alcohol mixed with human blood poisons the people who dwell here inside the red and blue houses. I am haunted by the many deaths inside the cold houses and outside the grotesque government buildings, corpses which die laughing, gruesome deaths of starving dogs. Always when I turn and look around carefully at the glum houses lining the crooked streets, tracing our doomed destiny, a bleeding wound opens. A thikoloshe spirit bewitches the buildings. It goes into the backrooms of the houses with a big wooden spoon which drips a green liquid, climbs down a step or two into the water drain.

A dull voice coming from a hard-pressed student starts to remonstrate with a shabby looking beggar whose two hands droop by his side. The dark tall student then turns to address two girls about their failures in life. I feel sorry for the girls who are clearly frightened by the student's insanity. Then he gets distracted and begins to torment a small dog with spider's legs. I tell the two girls to run and never to be involved with the student again. I watch them as they escape the long arms of his demented spirit, finally free from the enchanting beauty of his madness.

Yesterday a carefree prostitute reclined on my chair. The woman was Sotho. She had been dragged along the ground, by a drunken monster, a grubby and shrivelled old man who wanted to make a public demonstration. Her grandmother opened a tiny okapi knife, leapt forward, tore down on the monster and gouged out his left eye. Granny was locked inside a tiny cell in solitude. Only her deranged stepdaughter visited her at maximum security prison in St. Albans.

I think back to my schooldays when I brought arithmetic into my wandering nights. I had often seen one legless man who moved around the streets of Bhlawa like a rolling ball, lifting the entire weight of his body off the ground with the strength of his arms. I once heard that his legs had been severed by a giant saw. My encounters with this man happened at night. I would be coming from somewhere, maybe from visiting Dumi or one of my friends at Nkomponi hostel, and there I would see this lonely man shuffling forward along the gravel street. He was a nocturnal being, a beggar who only came out in the evenings when the sun had cooled down low enough, to bargain for his food. He opened dustbins, examined their contents, withdrew a banana peel, licked the smooth skin inside, drew back in disgust, with a convulsion. At times he made a cackling sound, laughing out loud to signal his presence. He knocked against everything, tavern doors, vegetable carts, stationary vehicles and homeless people sleeping in the streets. He threw what he didn't want back into the pile of rubbish, or into the street to be examined more thoroughly by hungry dogs. He picked up empty cool-drink bottles from the heaps of trash lying in the streets and drank the dregs of liquids still left inside. He swung his torso in jerking arcs, oscillating in the air in a hypnotic motion perfectly timed like the wings of a giant clock. He pushed himself painfully forward in what looked like an effortless movement, gaining momentum with every swing of his legless body being kept up above the ground by his strong arms. His lower limbs were wrapped all around by black plastic rubbish bags.

I began to count the number of half rotations the legless fellow mustered per minute with each forceful jolt of his disembodied frame. Nine. Even though this odd number of jolts fascinated me, it troubled me greatly. I wanted him to make a greater effort, amassing the entire power of his biceps, and attain a perfect score of ten swings. One night I followed him, determined not to miss a single one. We were moving in complete darkness. A fear suddenly arose within me that the legless fellow might fail my numbers test. My buoyant spirit shrunk a little. I prayed for something to happen, a snapping membrane or a banging door, to distract him from his exhaustion. I silently prayed that Uko, the crying spirit who moans the dead, would prod him on his way, inspire him to move forward.

I stood there under the electric pole dead-tired, while the devastating night was changing by the minute. A blind beggar, absorbed in his thoughts, forced his way through the busy night. A struggling dog walked past and then came back towards me, first sniffing my shoes, then greeting me with his ludicrous face. Like all things that are infinitely seized and then dazzled by the magic of dying, I stood by and watched the dog disappear in front of my eyes, making a chilling howl as it turned slowly to face the green doors of a nondescript building. I had strayed into the mindless realm of izithunzela and other night witches. My eyes, accustomed to the dark night, could see the silhouette of a muted spirit that remained fully present nearby for something like an hour.

Quickly I looked down the soulless street to see if the legless man hadn't also disappeared. I was pleasantly surprised to notice that he was back with his movement, and was now almost gyrating almost, gathering speed at each receding step of the thin light. A solid hour after I had first seen him, I could now walk normally again, maintain a safe distance of six metres between us, careful not to disturb his massive dream. He entered a long dark passage in a nameless street. Right ahead of us there was a house with dim lighting. I could hear voices laughing. The house had no windows. I was determined not to be seen by any living human. I had followed the legless man around the township for about three hours, and I was tired. I joined the crowd who went back-and-forth between the hair saloons and the drinking dens, glad that the walls of the world hadn't yet collapsed on them.

Now I am at KwaNdokwenza, looking around in this dreary hostel room, where I am keeping myself low for a while, hiding from the comrades, looking like a wounded animal. At Red Location, outside Dolla's house, I stand and listen to talking corpses in the delightful trees lining Avenue A and Hoza Community Hall. The sun is aggressive. A frowning spirit seizes me by the shoulder so that I begin to shudder deeply, terrified of all the wailing bodies that are hidden, practically indistinguishable from one another, under the red zinc houses of Red Location.

Today I drag my feet to the horrible spaza shops at Mbizweni Square and join the long queues for bread. One dismal looking shop displays a mannequin of a white man in fashionable clothing, and outside it a poor girl with a thin little voice sings of her dead mother. She stretches out a tiny hand clumsily to receive money for food from the cautious-looking people around her, but nobody looks in her direction.

18

I wanted to run away from the township. I felt I was in a prison and my life was going nowhere. My behaviour was boringly old and I wore my clothes hurriedly and out of fashion. Most of the people around me were wearing stiff chains on their necks in the form of sweet smiles. When I looked at their faces some instinct hinted at me that death had already come to visit. Everyone, men and women had grown so old. All of them had become strangers or hungry beggars who crowded the cruel corners of the streets waiting for their last day. Many of them had been forced to boycott school when the slogan had been 'Liberation before education'.

Two of my attempts to join the working world come into my mind. The first was my job as a postman when I was still in secondary school. I walked all over Bhlawa delivering typewritten letters to writers and artists for the Imvaba Cultural Society led by the famous isiXhosa poet, Soya Mama. My job lasted only a few weeks, but in that short time my eyes were sharpened to the dereliction of black lives in all the houses I visited. The wiring of my nervous system was changed forever.

The second was an interview for a study bursary in East London while I was finishing high school in 1988. I had applied to a big company for a bursary and received an invitation to come to East London for an interview. I boarded a taxi, bustled and blundered my way to the City Lodge in Oxford Street East London, where the interview was going to be held. I was totally shocked to suddenly find myself in the midst of sophisticated and neat-looking white students, all with their nice ties and colourful school hats, looking so erudite and rich. I felt so out of place in the large rooms of the hotel that I wanted to cry. I was tired from the long taxi ride, hungry and looking dishevelled like a town beggar. As expected, nothing came of the interview. The innocent young white woman who asked me a few questions was dumbfounded by my appearance and my complete lack of interest in the proceedings.

When freedom came in 1994, I abandoned my name "Michael". I could not carry it around with me anymore. I was no longer able to bear the pretence and confusion that my parents had started unknowingly, by giving me an English name. I went up to an office of the new government in North End, stood in a line. When my turn came I looked up at the funny-looking woman with her long face like a camel, and asked her to remove my English name from the register. The camel woman was both surprised and troubled by my request, then wanted to know if I was willing to pay a lot of money to erase my birth name. "Your parents had good reasons for naming you Michael. It is a good Christian name and shows you come from a good family." There was no going back for me, good family or not. I gave her two hundred rands (this amount included a substantial tip) to rid myself of my English name for good.

By this time I was 26 years old, unemployed and already feeling cheated by life, never having worked for any business firm or organisation in Port Elizabeth. My peers were already respectable employees of Delta and VW in Port Elizabeth and Uitenhage. All I really wanted was to be a writer. I dreamt of writing a big book about Bhlawa. I read *City Press* and the *New Nation*, newspapers which fired my imagination of escape into the world of poets. My habits of reading and carrying books everywhere made my peers believe I was a mad boy. They began to move away from me, fearing the disease that possessed me. I walked the streets with an even pace like a firewalker, looking all the time forward. I sailed through the terror of growing up thoughtful and unafraid, unshaken by ordinary life. I was full of marvellous and yet torturous ideas. Something was always happening in my small world. Messages were always brought in the wind, my postman. Sometimes I saw things and signs in the sky and in the earth. I heard the soft rustlings of spirits hiding, harsh voices trapped in the gutters of the street.

What was my place in the so-called real world? One night in Bhlawa a drunk woman invited me into her house and showed me a tiny sofa to sit on. There on the fading wall of the house, behind the unhinged door and the drunk woman who swayed precariously like a stick, hung the proud certificate of a shy poet from a township school. The certificate was issued by me. From my backroom office in Madala Street I had begun to hand out certificates for the amazing poems that were written by school children every year. The drunk woman and her pensive boy were owners of one of these. I handed out prizes, pens, books and schoolbags to kids in schools. I did it to challenge the school system which was offensive towards the children of the township, always despising their development.

I sat in my office wearing a dark blue suit and a green tie, like a man who's just come from a funeral. There was a tremendous smell of a crematorium and its pyre coming from the furniture. I could never tell whether this wafting odour of death came from the wet floor whose timber was rotting slowly, a green fungus covering its old wood like a heavy blanket, or whether the smell drifted in from the dilapidated RDP cabin next door to us, where Tshupi, our drunken neighbour, lived alone, smoking his spliff of cannabis leaves. A phone line ran across the grey ceiling of my office and entered a tiny hole in the blue wall where it hid perpetually, conversing only with the damp spirits of the night, inhabiting the four metre square room with the green tiles like a toad. Death was all around.

19

The summer rain looks like it will pour down in the coming hour. The street gutter will soon be saturated with its merciless torrents. The wind shakes the dry leafless tree opposite our house in Madala Street. I don't know if I really want to go out and visit my friend Shepherd, the linocut artist in Chris Hani, or rather stay indoors. I wonder sometimes whether it is fear rather than curiosity that drives me with its invisible hands to walk the black streets of Bhlawa every day, exploring the secrets of the grey miniature houses.

I enter a narrow street which attracts the lice of our world and see a limping spirit followed by a hostile crowd of women coming out of a small house, boisterous and radiant, drawing attention to themselves by the drunken sounds of their voices. When the owner of the small house roars at the women for fussing and beating down on his creaking tables, a young man with a broken spirit prepares for a fight, a menacing knife in his hand. "You are one of them Tata! I warned you not to come here. You are not welcome. Go back to your country!" A tall woman starts to walk back towards the small crowd of cheering spectators, her bony fingers clutching a silent purse. The rest of the crowd begins to disperse. The tall woman says something to the owner, who fidgets and stutters, a wailing parrot perched like a Buddha statue on top of his balding head. A black cat appears in the small yard from nowhere and sips the blood which forms a lazy pool outside the rusted fence.

The tall woman is wearing a turban and an enormous ring on her left hand. Both lenses of her spectacles are cracked in the middle, hiding her eyes. She stands up from her chair just behind the guests' table, her hands trembling and hidden behind her back. "What is wrong with all of you kids? You gave us such a fright." Pointing at me she says, "And as for this curious boy who walks around with a stern silence, he must leave the house immediately!" I understand that the invisible spirits in the house are now talking to me directly. I look all over the blackened ceiling, trying to trace the source of a green light that has now invaded every crevice of the house, wiping away the dust which has settled on the tables and the chairs.

The guests are sitting at the table, singing, eating and talking. I can sense the night giving way and broken entities being born, giving some guests stern looks and others comical expressions. One fat man, who someone says is a cousin to the minister of police, jumps back foolishly and falls behind a long chair. A woman with a green eye approaches the glass cabinet in the lounge, bumping into me, unable to see the way forward. A sad looking young man with wild afro hair goes from corner to corner scrubbing the dirty walls. I watch a young girl with terrific speed in her feet stamping the floor and shouting savagely, "My feet, my feet! Everything hurts my feet!" The noisy guests freeze suddenly, remembering their shaven heads and their bare shoulders, where the hand of God just an hour ago had lain idly like a spider on a window.

The township is like a bitch on heat squirming on all fours. It is a hadeda's terrible groan, it is loathsome and hissing like a viper. In a street where a young female student has been raped violently by thugs, I meet a plaintive deacon who has been broken by evil. All dead things are completely familiar to him. His sick sister is lying on a hospital bed at Dora Nginza in Zwide. He stares for hours at an old photo of his two boys who have disappeared. He is deadly quiet. In the photo the missing twins look back at their father, at something or someone that they can no longer comprehend or see.

In Summerstrand I also had my wandering routines. I startled a sleeping hobo outside a mall that sold flowers. I tasted new things eaten in the yellow cabins and met a few beggars. Very little happened in my grim world. I infuriated my father by following the birds. I scared even the blind tramps and the weeping widows. "What a strange boy," everyone shouted, "always wandering the streets alone and talking to himself!" I wasn't bothered. I kept on looking and looking down the alleys and byways of the suspicious valley with blue and green lights. I followed a limping man with a white stick.

In Happy Valley in Summerstrand, surrounded all around by grand houses, everyone walked so slowly. They had protruding trunks like the bellies of sleeping buildings. Their chests were hemmed in as if they hid atrocities. They all craned their necks out of the buildings' windows. Stones rained down from the windows to stop me. I ran towards what looked like a forlorn church. Flying insects and other birds of the sky pounded its doors and roof. A gardener stood by and watched me in low spirits. A little mouse ran into a hole inside the church. I sat on the church stoep squinting my eyes from the blinding light of the sun and hid under an overhanging arch of a side room.

Next to the bus stop near Norwich I watched falcons descend with ease towards the busy pavements to collect bread crumbs. I was alone without a voice and my fears multiplied. I grew visibly weak. My soul diminished. I was losing consciousness of the humans around me. I heard the imaginations of reckless devils and hidden spirits.

20

At Taliban University I hated the attitude of the rich white kids, their sense of belonging and ownership of the entire university space. I abhorred the blatant demonstration of their power and money. They behaved like they were the only people at Taliban, and the blacks undeserving hoodlums and miscreants.

The whites would eat at the dining hall like death was coming very soon – hot chips, hamburgers, toasted sandwiches, pies, sausage rolls, samoosas – mountains of delicious food, and gobble all of it down, all the while laughing, talking, cuddling and kissing. After that they would drink Coke or orange juice. I would be standing or sitting dead tired in a quiet corner of the hall of death, devastated by hunger.

The white students remained ostentatious and aloof. They owned the sofas, chairs and tables of the dying hall at the Students Union. They did not depend on meal cards and meal tickets for their food. They carried loads of cash in their wallets. They ordered special meals from the food company which was promptly delivered to them in their beds on trays neatly covered by transparent plastic wraps. Studying at Taliban University to them was the same thing as going to a good hotel in dead town.

They argued with the white head chef and the black workers about the quality of the cooking all the time. They stood there in the queue, seemingly not yet ready to move on with their plates, and argued. I never once met a hungry white student. They were all full of themselves. They went to the hall of death to make new friends and fall in love. They wore sandals on their feet. Some walked barefoot like Zola Budd. The men always wore white or black shorts, their women, almost nothing. The township never prepared me for these kinds of physical and emotional onslaughts.

For three painful weeks, a young white girl pushed my hostel door to complain about anything – noises that she perceived were coming from the tiny radio on my study table, loud voices that she was sure she heard coming from people and other invisible spirits talking in my room. She scolded me in front of my friends and then turned around swiftly and walked away, banging the door behind her. Some days she would just burst into my room without knocking, wearing skimpy shorts or a towel around her waist, and would just stare down at me with scolding eyes, not saying anything. My friends would taunt me about her behaviour, suggesting that I make friends with her. I never mustered the courage to do that, not wanting the attention and the impending chaos.

Rich black students occupied a lower rung in the social ladder of Taliban, just below the Indians and Coloureds. They displayed their parents' money and influence differently. Their hostel rooms were small palaces of opulence and excess. They bought large music sets, colour TVs, microwaves, expensive fridges and deep freezes. They even bought prostitutes from the townships. They drove fast cars and held the noisiest parties on campus.

One night, sitting alone in front of the TV in the student

common room, puzzled by all that was happening around me, I saw Dumi with his friends walking past me straight into the women's dormitory. He was no longer the converted soul who preached about the second coming of Christ. He now owned a piece of the hellish world that was slowly coming into being, amassing the energy and beauty of gullible young minds to power its engines.

Growing up in Bhlawa I was taught to always respect the elderly but also to stand up and fight against the bullies in Red Location. I had listened to Bob Marley on my cassette player singing his revolutionary song, "Get up Stand up". At age fifteen I read Steve Biko's book *I Write What I Like,* which my friend Ngqayimbana had lent to me. I was learning powerful lessons of liberation. I knew from a very early age that I would never be comfortable with oppressors. I was on a path to challenging Taliban's racists. So when a white professor manipulated my examination results I confronted him and called him a racist thug.

I had been excluded from going into the next year at Taliban on academic grounds, which was suspicious. Only African students were treated in this manner by the university. I walked into another oppressor professor's office to remonstrate about my examination results. After hearing my story, this oppressor professor wanted to know if I was Xhosa. "Yes, by both my parents," I said, "and I can't do a thing about it, I'm also black by the way." I left Taliban after that, began to value myself more. Which I needed when I was admitted to Royal Throne University (RTU).

21

The hostel at RTU where I rent a double room with Andile, a law student, is known as Beirut. It's a triple storey building, old and weather-beaten, smelling of stale urine. Seedy graffiti is on the walls. A group of feral cats has also made this appalling building its home. Students, whores, farm workers, clerks in government offices, hobos and unemployed civilians from neighbouring villages occupy the three hundred makeshift double and single rooms in the hostel. Our room is located next to what used to be a grand foyer on the ground floor, right next to the main entrance.

Most rooms in Beirut Hostel don't have electricity. There is no running water inside the building. Residents use the public toilets in York Road. A murky light bulb gives a poor light in our room every night, making it difficult for me to see properly, let alone read a book. Being next to the foyer, civilians knock on our door to ask me about lodging as if we're the admin office. Everything and everyone who enters or leaves the building knocks loudly at my door to greet me or to leave messages for their lovers. Even the ghosts from the nearby villages, who haunt our rooms in the hostel, communicate and make friends with me this way.

RTU discriminates between rich and poor students. Those who reside in Beirut are poor, five or more share a single room. They arrived at this university confident of receiving a study loan from the bursary office, but were disappointed.

The prestige of one's family name counts in every corner of this institution. Students with connections and good family names go very far. They get loans, good lodging, pass with distinctions and secure top jobs in government service. Their fathers are often judges, lawyers, magistrates, engineers, bankers and medical doctors. Their mothers are prominent politicians, or senior lecturers and high ranking officials at RTU. I am revolted by their obscene tastes and their grotesque standards of living. I am destroyed by their universal lies, thieves who steal nubile ideas and contribute nothing. Every oppressor professor defiles a young girl in her gullible state and steals her money.

I have not eaten meat for three weeks. I survived by eating carrots, rice and beetroot. Last month when I ate meat I became sick for days. I lay in my bed groaning. My room mate Andile slips into my side of the room, fiddles inside the wardrobe for a minute and pulls out a dark green bottle with a foul smell. He pours the stinking liquid into the cup and hands it over to me in my bed. "Here, drink this if you plan to go on living," Andile tells me quietly, "otherwise, prepare for a painful death."

A shove in the back awakens me. It is almost supper time. Andile holds his plate and spoon in his hand and begs me to go with him to the dining hall of death. I refuse. I know I would be served like a king by the ghosts in death hall if my father had been a minister of a church, or even a pilot flying an aeroplane. Favourable treatment to beggars only happens when they have good money to buy a meal ticket. You would then be free to eat all your meals in the dying hall, always leaving food in your plate to show you are not starving. Thinking about the long queue at that place weakens my hunger. I decide to stay behind and cook rice. After betting on a winning horse on the weekend, I was able to go to Spargs grocery shop and buy myself a bag of potatoes and Jabula soup. I want to celebrate. I think about my father who died a year ago. He always discouraged me from betting, saying it was the devil's plan to keep black people poor.

Mtheza knocks at my door and comes in. I am shocked at how quick he has grown thin. He looks completely malnourished. He says the last cooked meal he ate was two weeks ago. He has been starving slowly the entire time. A woman that he fell in love with a long time ago in Bizana had given him R20 in town. The first things that came into his mind were cigarettes and a cold glass of beer. He saved R10 of the money to buy himself bread and has been surviving the entire time on bread and water. Starch upsets his stomach. He is always constipated and last night when he went to the public toilets to shit, there were traces of blood on the toilet paper.

I put my two plate stove on my study desk to begin to cook rice. Mtheza sits on my bed, his back leaning against the wall, feet dangling. He closes his eyes. He looks very weak. His face is pale as though all the blood has been removed from the veins.

"What is taking you so long Mxo to cook rice, or are you cooking impundulu?" Mtheza asks, his eyes still closed but his head facing the ceiling. I peel the three potatoes that I will eat with the rice. I know that it is his hungry stomach that is talking to me. Not his haunted spirit.

Andile enters the room with his new girlfriend, Titi. They

quickly go to their side of the room. I hear the soft noise from the sagging springs of Andile's bed and conclude that he is sitting on the bed with Titi. Each side has only a single iron bed, a study table, a tiny wardrobe and a chair. I hear them breathing quietly.

I'm awoken by the loud groans of Andile and Titi tearing the night apart with angry sounds, mixing hot bodily fluids. Their lovemaking is like the shrieking of the feral cats outside. He only has this tiny bed to sing his nightly dirges to Titi. He tells me that time is running out for them. I wonder how, for both of them are barely into their twenties. He wants to marry Titi, but first must make sure she can bear him an indlalifa (heir). Sometimes when I see Andile and Titi cuddling in our double room, I go out and sleep on the old couch in the passage upstairs.

I don't have a girlfriend though I've been eyeing this pretty girl who lives in a third floor room. She works as a butcher's assistant in town. Nevertheless, I'm afraid of the maintenance costs that she will bring to me. Shoes, cell phones, hair styles, fake nails, designer clothes. The list of items necessary to love a black woman goes on and on. My poverty will multiply three times with a girlfriend. The urge for my indlalifa is weak. I have nothing to leave to anyone.

At RTU's death kitchens there is always a hostile atmosphere, with hungry students fighting with the workers over food. I am disgusted by the hunger, and my own hunger makes me very angry. The gogo ghosts who cook our food in the kitchen are hateful and cruel towards emaciated students. They order them around, constantly bullying and taunting the weak ones. "Bring your own plates and spoons when you come to eat! You steal our cutlery," says the senior cooking crook.

I always go to the dining hall as late as possible, minutes before closing time, to avoid the big rush. The cooking crooks are more calm at that hour but their sharp tongues are just as biting. "Why do you come late? Do you think you are special that you can sit here alone and make us wait for you to finish your food? Next time we will leave nothing for you in the kitchen!" A few days later I go to the dining hall with my shining pot to get my supper. "Take your stupid helmet away! We are not going serve you until you come back with a plate!"

22

Ten years ago I was accepted as a 'mature' student in creative writing, I stopped dreaming and became alert. I could no longer fall asleep. I checked my emails. There it was, Rogues University confirming my enrolment as a student. I could even dare now to dream of writing my heretic book of flowers and birds.

The false oppressor professor smiles, a dirty smile. He asks for a slice of bread and lime juice from the waitress in the bleary canteen. Outside, from the other entrance where none of the diners can see me, I can see a bloody sunrise in the distance. I am hungry. I haven't eaten a decent meal in days. I go to the lecture halls quiet and pensive, expecting any minute some skullduggery to happen, a fatal slip on the concrete stairs of the old university, followed by death from lack of food or oxygen. Even at Rogues University, some students go for days with nothing in their stomachs.

Every night, when the doors of the canteen close after supper, the prof crawls back to his tidy office to write a novel about sick animals in the rain forests. It is full of apocalyptic lines: *Rain forests have no sky. There are horses and marksmen in the plains. Old men with the mark of swords on their arms and faces quietly face the wind. From the deep gorges swallows, the size of twenty elephants, fly slowly upwards, closer to the moon. A small man with an axe dripping a fallen god's blood goes into the rain forests to pray.*

The oppressor professor's students stand behind him in the queue in the canteen and join him in conversation. They flatter him. The women wear makeup. Their naked breasts show through their skimpy tops, bulging outwards. Some wait patiently outside, sitting on the benches of the corridor waiting their turn to meet their saviour. The quest for a degree has been complicated by madness. Like powerful dogs that have been domesticated by man over many centuries, professors like mating. And they are good at it, always ogling at every puberty-charged student, boy or girl. These educated bastards don't discriminate between the sexes. Tonight the gentleman sleeps with a man. The following afternoon, after a long lecture which he stammered his way through, he goes and sleeps with the blonde girl. They are spewing out degrees that are tenderized by heated sex and their chronic madness.

I emerged from Rogues with an MA despite everything that was going on around me – the supervision wars among lustful teachers, the executions of revolutionary poets, and the betrayals by gullible spirits. Perhaps I could now become a teacher in my township with two shoes and a black pen.

The MA enabled me to register for a PhD. Over two years I worked on my thesis on ukuthetha and the talking songs of maskandi, until one day prof told me that my whole approach was wrong. He says I put too much heart into my words. "Don't put emphasis on feelings, Mxolisi," he says, "they will destroy you. Give me your brain. Your heart will only deceive you."
"I don't believe in the rational world," I tell him.
"What do you believe in then?" he asks me.

"I don't believe in anything that wants to destroy the world. That's what it means to be human."

I deregister. I will not believe his crap. It spells endless disaster. It is too sanitised, like lies dressed in clean clothes. I leave these monsters of my thoughts in the prof's brain. At graduation I see all the oppressor professors lining up there on the stairs to receive bloody degrees from the VC. One of them, with a bowler hat and a long gown, approaches me in the corridor of the long canteen wearing a blue scarf and a fake smile. He is a drug mule, that I can see. And he has slept with all the woman students. I take a side exit trying to foul his penchant for human blood. He barks silently. I decided years ago to cut no deals with my oppressor professors. So many of them wish me dead. History in their books also wishes me dead. I carry within myself stories that many people wish were forgotten.

I've noticed the dignity of titles at the university. Men and women make money from them. I now insist to be addressed as Bhodlinja, Bdj. for short, my traditional title, especially here inside the corridors of power. I ventured forward towards the VC's office. All his skeletons were in the right places, in the closets and behind doors. I was reminded of my deep hatred of the world. Doing the course was a mistake, a project really meant for slaves. Thanks god, I could have drowned in somebody's piss! The university corridor leads nowhere.

Xoli, the girl who lives in a flat just opposite mine, is angry that I even entertained the conversation with prof. "Your weakness comes from being rejected by your family in your teens. You are always weakened by 'I love you's'. You are dead in your underpants, Mxolisi. Start going to church. Pray for yourself. You are nothing without God." The Zimbabwean girl, Leti, who helps with my chickens, is a healer. From a young age she was sent to hospitals in Zim to heal the sick. I'll ask her tomorrow to prepare me an iyeza to ward off my bad spirits, starting with prof. She has been sent to look after my chickens for a reason.

Nobody owns me. Even during those times when everyone tried to buy my soul with thirty pieces of silver, I stood firm and rejected their advances. I stayed with my freedom. Slavery comes in many disguises, sometimes dressed in the solid clothes of educated men, inside the certified copies of their complicated CVs. Every school I went to tried to tamper with my freedom. Every institution of higher learning wanted to make a wounded man out of my scapular and my skull. Deceitful priests prayed hard to imprison my ribs. Warmongers ransacked my mind to drain it of its sweetest colours. Women seduced me with voluptuous words. Daggers and thugs came out. Forty knives emerged from sore scars and wounded forests to ridicule my innocence. When my turn came to depart from the house of sins and unholy matrimonies, they unshackled sorrow to devour my limbs.

23

A one roomed house appeared one morning in Madala Street. It was not there the previous night. Nobody had seen or even heard the boisterous noise of construction work. It seems this was not an isolated case. No one knew what to do except to report the apparitions of the ghosts and their makeshift houses to the ward councillor. The ward councillor announced that the undocumented houses would be abolished by the municipality. Because it was nearly time for elections, he decreed that the work of demolishing the mysterious structures would commence soon after the voting in of the new council. But the matter of the unknown visitors and their curious structures was not that simple. No, this was not the work of the government nor of the municipality. It was the work of the devil and his witches.

Two weeks later, the one roomed house in Madala suddenly disappeared under equally mysterious circumstances. A number of official events seemed to be linked to this new scandal. First the mayor of the city, Mr Linda, drove by the main road leading to Bhlawa with a long convoy of cars. Then a political party demanded land from the municipality to build more houses. The mayor was going to Centenary Hall to address a group of agitated workers and young people from jobs summit organised by Harambee, a youth employment agency. The workers were demanding living wages and better working conditions from their bosses.

Meanwhile out in the streets the residents were busy

burning tyres and singing freedom songs,

Umam' uyajabula	My mother becomes elated
Xa ndihleli phezu kwendlu kaLinda	When I sit on top of Mr Linda's house
Umam' uyajabula	She becomes elated
Umam' uyajabula	She becomes happy
Jabula mama	Mother, celebrate with me
Jabula mama	Rejoice
Jabula mama	And celebrate

Something else happened that day that disturbed the whole township. The excitable young driver of a Quantum taxi drove straight into the front wall of a Somali spaza shop in Dora Street. The shopkeeper, a middle-aged man with a solemn face and a long white beard like a bird, called for reinforcements on his cellphone. In a short space of about ten minutes eight vehicles driven by Somali marksmen and other rich businessmen of Islamic descent from Korsten drove into the township brandishing bazookas and R4 rifles. They looked utterly fearsome, like the apartheid military. Someone said these guys had been trained in the wars in Somalia and Sudan and Burundi. They looked like people who have had enough of death, their long robes and white shirts worn loosely as if they had been rudely awoken from a bad dream. They were mute as horses. They were war veterans who had decimated tribes and brought nations to their knees.

A scuffle began between the men from the Hamba Taxi Association and the Somalis who were threatening to shoot the taxi owners and their drivers. A taxi was quickly set alight by the Somalis. The taxi bosses jumped into a Mercedes Benz parked nearby and disappeared from the scene, leaving the spectators, including young kids going to school, petrified on the street, wondering whether to continue with their normal day or go back to their homes where they would crouch safely inside.

I returned to the streets of dead town the following day to find the gullible spirits in a jovial mood. They were so happy that tears ran down their faces. They had agreed on an ambitious plan to build thousands of houses to celebrate their chief who died years ago in a small hut the size of a peanut. A secret ballot confirmed a landslide victory for the new project: 105 votes to 8. The work of building the first five hundred houses was going to be beamed to TV screens in every house in the country. It was going to be watched by one-eyed beggars, witches and their children, thieves and murderers, all of them loyal members of dead town. A team of building experts was quickly assembled. Builders came from all walks of life to erect massive chambers and underground tunnels and tombs that swallowed the earth. A huge rod tunnelled its way through a mountain and gouged through the rocky terrain, steaming into the hard ground and spilling out rocks and sewerage. A tower with high walls was built to monitor the work which continued each day uninterrupted in 24-hour shifts.

On the verandas of the completed five hundred houses, dead spirits were seen dancing and singing. They celebrated loudly when a particularly stubborn granite rock obstructing the view of the main road was uprooted by two digging machines. Outside a spaza shop which sold bread and takeaway food to the builders, street children and other homeless people were bundled by a group of revellers into a steel cage, forced into the back of a truck and driven away.

That same day a notorious gintza was to be buried at Veeplaas. Several shots were fired into the air by gang members, who were honouring their fallen colleague. Shots were also fired off by comrades from the workers' party, who were intimidating the mayor's convoy of cars. When this commotion had died down, someone reported hearing a deafening sound, like of two trucks colliding or an earthquake.

I was depressed by the violence and all these strange events in our township. One morning I wandered near the railway bridge and met a stranger, his name was Loliwe. We talked about the series of unfortunate and weird occurrences. We concluded that undocumented and unknown people had arrived, and rows of buildings appeared all over the township, seemingly from nowhere, with no logical reason, built by the devil. Some buildings had crawled out of the ground and appeared in empty fields, some right in the middle of small streets, seemingly bent to join existing homes. Some of these houses arrived fully furnished, others came empty and naked as caves. Loliwe was an old man who lived with his two grandsons in Jabavu Street. He had noticed that the one roomed house in Madala Street had disappeared and he knew about the scandals with the undocumented houses.

Loliwe told me another strange story. A few feet across from where we were standing, over the railway line, was eMpelazwe, a tract of land where the township ended violently, and the town of the dead began. Girls from the township were being ambushed daily at 2 a.m. by either amagqwirha or the South African police and flown on brooms and mops to eBhakubha and eGwadana, the towns of the witches, at 600 kilometres an hour.

One evening, while Loliwe was coming from church, an isithunzela with a cup hat and terrible teeth confronted him and blocked his path. Loliwe noticed a nearby tavern and ducked inside. An unfathomable music played loudly inside the tavern. He emerged from a tiny kitchen inside the house and entered a different world of elevated doorways, long passages and blinding mirrors. In one room, which looked like it could have been a holding cell for immigrants who had no papers, a cascading white light streamed down from the ceiling towards the ground. On the floor a group of small children prepared their insurrection against the owners of the pub. The children stuck out their tongues and drew on the floor to keep away the hideous corpses of the house – drunkards, moths, house flies, visiting mayors, students, girls, garden boys, women with aprons, pastors with fiery sermons, veterinary surgeons, gangstas and cockroaches.

In the big belly of this underground universe were Bhakubha and Gwadana, the two cities invisible to the naked eye, inhabited by ghoulish witches and other executioners. The outbuildings in the yard of the tavern house, which was bigger than two rugby fields, were arranged like luminous clouds to face the sun. Nearby one hut an initiate was busy stoking the flames of a mountainous brazier that was glowing fiercely like a shooting star.

Loliwe told me that his uncle Skuta, a consumptive atheist, had walked with his dog across a mealie field until he came to a cross on the road. There he prayed to be saved from the terrifying witches of Gwadana. That same week Skuta disappeared from Bhlawa without a trace. A medicine man said he had been jailed in Gadwana by the witches. I shuddered to think about Skuta's fate on the last night of the yearly funeral called Easter.

Loliwe told me he had sped off towards a chapel with a falling cross having devised an elaborate plan to bargain with the bodyguards and graveyard wardens in the tavern to secure Skuta's release. His idea involved marrying one of the witches and paying twenty cows for her lobola. But it was not welcomed by the witches. They sat on a couch and drank a strong concoction made of the bitter leaves of a wild fruit. They asked him to leave the tavern of whores immediately. The rotting smell of a dead dog on the railway line added to the putrid smell of the witches' house. It signalled to the world the massacre of the people in the township.

After three hours of listening to Loliwe and his stories, I had grown fifty times hungry. Across the busy highway, from one of the Chinese shops in Deal Party, an appetising smell of potato chips, russian polony and amagwinya was coming towards me, drifting towards the railway station with the wind. A train to Johannesburg sounded a siren. A ticket inspector stood on guard and roamed its cabins. Working men crowded the railway station and chased after their dreams.

Even before I was a teenager, I had been fascinated by

the invisible world of the dead. I remember standing midway between the Constantia mall and the chemist shop, watching labourers work in the burning sun. At the centre of the mall there were long escalators which climbed upwards towards heaven. Inside the building were glass walls, shops crowded with the enticing voices of seductresses and invisible spirits. There was also a place right in the middle of the mall where a mirage of streaming lights formed a gigantic column. The fascinating illusion created by the huge pillar of lights played out just opposite the floating escalators. Troubled folks from the township often stood or passed by shivering, taken aback by the waterfall that flowed eerily downwards along the perpendicular column, towards the centre of the earth.

The mischievous spirits of our dead town kept on at me. In Grogro, just outside Bhlawa, I came across a church that had no building. All its worshippers wore white clothes. They stood and prayed in a circle. I could not join them in their prayers for the dead for I had no alms, no offering to calm the sect's noisy voices. Nevertheless I kept singing by myself away from everyone. The dead paraded the margins of the empty circle of the church only coming out at night to torture the township with their ancient songs. They looked for me in the streets, but could not find me.

I met an elder who was frowning, throwing his trembling hands all over and shivering. He was shouting out the indignity of living in the sinking ship of the township on behalf of everyone, from street dwellers to dogs to people who sold insurance for the white companies in dead town. He said the dim-witted police wanted to kill him. "Old man you have a house, a wife and five children. Go home and don't be involved in politics." After a long time of reflection, the elder's cheeks quivered and his misty eyes looked down the street contemplating a bygone time. He shuffled his old feet forward and went off to share heretical tales with widowed women and motherless children.

The dead men used to call out to me to join them in their schemes. I refused to listen. I refuted their deadly world and did not go. They persisted. I stopped. I listened. I drank water from a tap in a public toilet in a dirty street where only black people were allowed, close to a green sign that said "Nie-Blanke". Just opposite that sign there was another one handwritten in bold black letters which read, "Caution Beware Of Natives". I tasted an apple from a withered garden.

24

Every day I see myself abandoning my house and becoming invisible. I leave my life behind – my wife, my clothes, my books and other useless possessions that weigh down on me in internal misery. I am walking away from everything. My wife has laid down a mat at the front door of our house where beggars knock to ask for bread. Some days I feel sympathy for the beggars and give them food. When I am pressed for time and must rush to feed my chickens, I chase the disorderly beggars away. I dress myself in boots and a grey shirt and with a firm intransigence leave the house without saying a word to anyone.

Yesterday I heard a loud and insistent noise at my gate. The howling human voice sounded desperate. I went to check its source. I found Silo standing there, the young man who cleans our garden, cuts the grass, picks up papers. He knows I am at home. He sees the kitchen window open. I become upset when I see Silo's bright and hopeful face. It can't be anything good.

"Silo, I told you to only come on weekends. You can't just drop in anytime you like and ask to clean the garden. I told you last time, I have no jobs for you this month. Please come month end."

He looks down for a minute, disappointed. Then he adds quickly, "Don't you have R2 with you? I want to buy sliced polony."

I turn around and go back to the house, moaning out loudly. I take the last R5 I have in the sideboard, go back outside to face my tormentor.

"Now here's R5. But clean the yard first."

I make him a sandwich and call him to eat. He confronts me after eating.

"You did not add sugar to the tea."

"I'm sorry Silo, my wife and I don't use sugar, and there is nothing in the house now."

"OK, I will fix the tea endlini."

"What are you talking about?"

"I'm talking about my tea. I have sugar at home. The tea is nice. I will pour it into my drinking bottle and warm it when I'm at home."

The faces of the beggars in my street are creased hard with questions. Their lives are empty histories. Inside their veins flow terrible rivers. All kinds of convicts are locked carefully behind bars below that ocean of silence. I try very hard to avoid conversations with them. That is why it's better to leave my house early in the morning.

Like the beggars, I am safer in the street. In the house you are easy prey for them when they do their daily rounds in the mornings, between 8 and 11 a.m. They study the houses carefully for any signs of people, saying to themselves:

"The windows are open."

"The car is parked outside."

"The door is open."

"The radio is playing."

"There is a smell of food cooking."

All these are important indicators to beggars. They exchange a wealth of information about whether or not to go and knock on the door of a house to beg for food. The routine of begging is easy – a cap squashed tightly in one hand, a slight dropping of the shoulders, a leaning or stooping forward, an inaudible voice, looking down on the ground and avoiding eye contact with the victim. Once everything has been ascertained by an experienced beggar, that is, a target has been verified by instinct and found ready for taking, the thought rushes to the beggar's head: "Great heavens, what good luck! Let me take my chances now and go and howl at the front door. They will definitely come out sometime. They won't be able to stomach my desperation."

I resolutely go out early from the house to avoid this drama, as soon as my wife leaves, to be with the chickens at my township farm. It is much safer there, closer to the abandoned veld.

I work hard in my blue spaza container in Motherwell. Every day I leave home at six in the morning and come back late in the evening. When I speak of looking for another job, Noxolo replies to me half-mockingly, as if she had no personal interest in my plans. The spaza sells sandwiches to schoolchildren, drinka-pops, loose cigarettes, vetkoeks and airtime. My vetkoek section is growing too slowly. The young girl who manages the hot foods clearly doesn't know what she is doing. Our customers complain every day.

I have longed to go away from Bhlawa but something has always held me back. Besides I have no money to leave. Confusion pours into my heart and I scramble around the back rooms of my existence hardly knowing which direction to take, what action would allow me to escape.

One calm evening I stopped protesting. I was drinking a

cold glass of beer in my bedroom. Ntosh, the girl who was living with me at the time, called out to me in a lively voice, "Mxolisi, can you see what is becoming of your life? You should get a job soon. The municipality has vacancies. Why don't you apply? Surely you will get something."

Ntosh might have been right, but that wouldn't have solved my problems. My problems live in my blood, like old trees with stubborn roots. I doubt they will ever go away.

One of my friends is a young man named Siza, newly-released from St. Albans Prison with his dark soul intact. He does not talk much about his previous life. But from the creases under his eyes, and from the deep-set silence that his soul exudes all the time, I gather that his perturbed spirit has seen and experienced the worst in life. Siza surprised me with a question the first day he came over to the container.

"Don't you remember me?"

I didn't recognise him. I see new faces every day, people who try to sell to me all kinds of suspicious articles: electric kettles, laptops, locks, aprons, women's underwear, sprinklers, cooking utensils, knives, shoes, DVDs, car parts.

"No, I don't remember you from anywhere."

"But Taima, you read poems to us in prison in 2005. I was in St. Albans when you came to talk about poems."

Close to my container in Motherwell is the huge Spar complex. Inside the grotesque building, Chinese and white men look over the customers with puzzlement on their faces as if they were encountering aliens arriving there for their first dark mission. From the angry streets I see the devastation of the Motherwell community – elderly women who carry bags of every kind of thing imaginable: food, medicine, meat, live chickens, girls' socks. Every day they carry these things to the corner stalls in the cold rainy street in Umnulu and sell their life's possessions.

In Motherwell, as in many townships in our country, the streets, the dying municipal street-lights, the wasted municipal buildings and the wandering gutter animals are consumed in the strange laughter of drugs and angry parties. Here life pursues incomprehensible rhythms and rattles, surrounded by death and miraculous hindrances. And do not be surprised by the gymnosperm of lovers!

Here in Motherwell every person in every household sways a flag to say, "We are the radiant spirits of a new struggle. Our silence resonates with our anger." It is not surprising at all to see these days a fifteen-year-old girl or boy drinking beer in the street, at midday with the sun shining, in full view of everyone sipping drunkenly away, maybe also chatting up some friend who's also drunk or drugged.

I see no difference between the parliament of elites and the corrupt universities of the blind. At least the shipping containers that line the streets serve the poor people their daily needs. Today I'll go to my awkward looking marine container in the streets in Motherwell to teach hopeless and poor youths about computers and how to use them. I keep my religious life there, far away from everything and everyone, inside my blue sailing ship where life blurs to dimness within the space of one minute. There are drafts of poems on the table, hard words that are invaded by insects needing the smell of earth to calm their daily routines. I'll rummage through my notebooks and look for the seed-rains and flowers to startle the January sleep

from my eyes. In Motherwell I can live like everyone. I sleep
with the sky. I keep the mantle of the evening, deliver hope
like a leaf to the world.

25

A man named Dan, who preys on widowed women, has wormed his way into my mother's purse. I confront this man in Funde Street. There's a big spectacle. He draws out a bayonet and lunges forward towards me to strike, wielding the blade. I step to one side to avoid it. He chases me down the street loudly bawling sharp curses. I report the attack to the police in Bhlawa. I put down a short statement. A detective tells me I will receive a WhatsApp message with my case number. The two policemen in the tiny office appear extremely bored with life.

The old lady says I must be careful around Dan. "You will die. Be careful." Tomorrow I have called a meeting with the elders in the family. We are battling my mother's ill health. Her back pains have come back with some vengeance. She has been to the clinic. They gave her medicine, but told us that very little can be done. Her age is the main contributing factor. The pills give her no relief. She cries morning to evening, I don't know long she can do this. At the clinic we learn from a doctor that she has dementia. I think of the many times when she has denied something that she did or said, forgotten the names of people who visit her, not know where she left her bank card, or seen invisible insects and animals. Dan's wily visits to our house start to make sense.

I am learning to walk again slowly after the beating I got from a drunk gintza outside the tavern. I was also drunk by the way. I had no business to talk sweet words to the beautiful girl in the tavern. I walk like a weasel. I am learning to talk intelligibly, but my words have no direction. They spill out of my mouth like vomit, green and smelling. My poems are ways to try to bury myself underground slowly, like an ant. I hasten my struggle to die every day. It's always the same thing, a short life with a bland smile.

I decide to go and see Dolla. He walks out of his sunless room carrying a heavy canvas painting. Wet paint trails like a dog's saliva down his coarse hands. He does not look at me but continues straight towards the bus shelter opposite KwaSigxabhayi Church, where a scrawny girl sits on a tomato box in the middle of the street talking with Charlie, his next door neighbour. Both Charlie and Dolla are wearing flip-flops. They all begin to swear violently at each other until the girl lifts her skirt up and swears by her dead mother in her grave.

Dolla turns back noticeably shaken. He asks for a cigarette from Charlie who says, "What were you thinking mtshan' am? All these whoreish township girls are like this. You play them, they destroy your paintings." I look at the young woman who is hardly nineteen, licking her lips and rolling up her sleeves, clearly strongly agitated.

"Tell Phumla about me. Does she know anything about Kwazakhele girls? She does not want to know me", the girl warns Dolla loudly, her morning bhabhalaza priming her to start another brawl.

"Why do you always treat women like this?" I hear Charlie asking.

"They are pigs", Dolla retorts crudely.

Later in Dolla's sitting room Charlie asks, "What will

happen to her?"

Dolla leans with his back on a primus stove stuffed on the table, shuffling his feet over the damp wood floor. "Aya will pay for the damaged paintings. I will see to it. Watch out. I will not let another bitch ruin my hard work."

In the street I'm being followed by a limping dog. The animal has been flogged right through its skin like so many domestic creatures before it, and never barked. It has swollen welts and a barbarous stitch on the head that is unbearable to look at. Dogs whose blindness is exaggerated by the amount of sulphur in their blood and the swelling of death can easily abandon life. They die heedlessly, lost like lemmings in the wild. They turn their backs on life and become subjects of endless gossip. Later in their deaths, inside their graves, they are restored to their animal splendour, and begin to bark like healthy vicious animals.

A bishop and two nuns are moving around the yard of the Catholic Church in Phendla Street displaying a huge cross. Their actions bewilder the residents and upset beer drinkers who frequent the shebeens on weekends. The three clerics invite homeless dwellers and other lost souls to the House of the Lord to join them in their victorious walk to Calvary. I detect that many people feel awkward and ashamed to join the proverbial march to Zion. "Well, what are you waiting for, mzalwane? The Lord of Israel is waiting for you, my friend," the bishop says bluntly.

A floating spirit with a black hat emerges out of nowhere looking hurt, and immediately berates me: "Did you read your books or stay up all night dreaming? Did you say your prayers to the NEXT WORLD? Mxolisi, you are a foolish boy. You don't understand anything. Must I say life is like a boy who crosses the road in the dark? His voice is small. His movements are all so slow. He listens to the dark world around him. Everything is all there in that moment. His truth to be borne alone. And to cross the dark streets of the world alone."

I think of Mambush, the rock-drill operator of Marikana, wrapped in a green blanket, who fought bravely against an intoxicated spirit and Africa became quiet. Didn't that signal the start of everybody's exile? Mambush told them "We are going to kill each other today," but nobody listened. He fed on enmity and the sound of guns. He grew alone with no infernal beast inside, no parent, no sibling, no school, no happy childhood photographs. Fire, magic and death surrounded him in puberty.

That morning on a koppie was as bad as any other in history. The police were naïve. At any moment they could go insane. Evil things flourish inside people when their truth dies. Murder grows from deep in the earth. Vanity and cruel words surface above the black soil and torment everyone. Which dictators were we all being led to?

26

One Sunday morning many years ago, a preacher named Nongalwana told me that I must stop with my questions. We were sitting under a tree as the day was burning hot. Nongalwana had just come from delivering a sermon in church. He was still flushed with excitement. He told me official men in suits and ties were seated in an important meeting just next door to us. When the officials swallowed the cake the lady in tight jeans served to them, they must not be disturbed.

"Mxolisi, no one will walk away from the events of the township unscathed," Nongalwana said to me, while putting his hand in one of his pockets, and drawing out a handkerchief. "At this rate," he concluded, "nobody will be spared. Nothing will stop anything from happening."
I remained seated on the creaking wooden bench puzzled by Nongalwana's words. I tried to say something in return, but Nongalwana wouldn't let me. When he noticed that something was bothering me, he ordered in a firm voice, "You must listen to me, my son. Do you hear anything at all? Is not all the softness of God's Kingdom knocking on your door?"
Then he added dramatically, "Open the door! Free your soul! Abandon your sinful ways! Jesus was nailed on the cross to free you from hell!"

Nongalwana's words left me shuddering all over. After that talk with him under the tree, I woke up every morning feeling I must be somewhere, I must do something.

"What?"

"Where?"

Things began and ended for me right under that very same tree where we were sitting. That was my favourite spot to sit idly and consider my life in relation to the beggars. My dilemmas were reflected in the eyes of the beggars, in what they saw in the world, how they understood their humanity. How were we going to live with ourselves? The streets were places of violent sounds, guns firing, screams, birth howls, taxis speeding, dead souls blasting off into empty space. Nobody was being tortured by the comrades or violated by the police, yet in Grogro children were living in the streets, like dogs, sleeping out in the open bush or under bus shelters, battling to find food. Life stood still. Under my tree I could always discern the death of a beggar from miles away, hear the screams of perilous lives that were jailed in prison.

Through all my dilemmas my poems were a road towards somewhere, an escape towards a church building, a grave, a choirmaster with little angels singing softly, a soldier's dungeon, a roulette table where used angels and white balls rolled endlessly. Sitting under the tree listening to Nongalwana, I felt like a bird trapped inside a cage. My meeting under the tree with Nongalwana reminded me of the TV serial *Star Trek*. A voice message sent to the galactic space ship would instruct the Station Commander to beam him up, and Captain Kirk would be seen in the following scene standing next to an alien or a dragon in a lost world.

I found our street more taciturn than ever. Had I known early that Nongalwana was a pastor, I would have abandoned

124

my usual spot under the tree immediately, despite the blistering heat of the sun. I had no bones for self-righteous predators like Nongalwana. The smell of violence in the township was too much. I looked around. Outside the four damaged walls of my prison cage there was one more road waiting – the one that led to Veeplaas.

I knew that Nongalwana was talking about something that made sense to him. He was imagining a different universe whose characteristics and longings were impartial, and exhibited ostensibly, and in public, a worthless cause. His words were not addressing broken souls like those of the beggars.

"Be careful of what you say to the beggars," I told him. "Your message is of the church not their world."

Nongalwana did not understand the need for solitude and being alone.

"Wait for me here until midday when I will come with my parish to spread the news of the second coming," he said.

I had read many books written in poor people's faces, including a few from Nongalwana's bible. Malice swelled compulsively on earth, the same way as it overwhelmed the beggars. That was why the people in the streets always discussed the former days of the sun. Why the tramp walked towards the spaza shop with three missing fingers. Everything that I wrote those days asked questions for which there were no answers.

27

One day a thin sickly looking coloured man called Mollie came to see me in my office. I could not ascertain if his pale skin came from Malayan descent or from Kaapse coloured roots. This pallid man was an official of the Department of Water Affairs and Forestry in the Western Cape. He drove from Cape Town to visit shoal and abalone fishermen who toiled for their subsistence at Swartkops estuary, near Motherwell. A lot was being bandied about in the news about the government introducing new fishing laws because South Africa had become a new country. I had written a short letter to the department asking if they could give any support to these men who fished by throwing their lines into the middle of a rising sea, standing firm on unsteady boats, or holding steady on their naked limbs in the water, defying death in order to put food on their tables.

Mollie told me that I could help the fishermen by joining them in their boats. He believed that was the only way of befriending them. He wanted me to teach them how to write their names, read some fishing books and pamphlets from the department, and do basic arithmetic. I was not very eager to join the fishing trade. Nevertheless I went. Out at sea a mild storm was brewing up. I listened carefully to the sound of a flaunted rainbow in the sky and heard the condescending message of a sea that was harnessing its black winds. When the sea's agony became too much for me to bear alone, all by myself among the group of absolutely loud and demented fishermen, I became nauseous. I then began to paddle recklessly to the shore with a boy who was helping me in a raft to escape the creepy seafarers and their grandiose behaviour.

Later that day, I saw the fishermen and other horned spirits drifting calmly towards the shore in their vessel. From the safety of the shore, I could still see a few of the men remaining steadfast at their posts in the middle of the sea, standing firm on their limbs with their fishing lines, defying the cruel hand of death. I went away from the bleak port to the poor town of Swartkops to wander about mindlessly and alone in a street like a stray dog. I saw in the devastating harbour with the small town's ten fishing boats, tons of rotting fish, nets, tremendous paddles and a long willow rod that had been dislodged from the base of a sunken raft. In a cabin where the bodies of sardines and other small fish had been cut and dumped in the shadows of a room, I found a squad of fishermen and their noisy women brandishing the night with their rage. "Dead town has forgotten about us," the men and women retorted. We were sitting down to drink the blackest coffee I had ever seen. The men had not shaved in months. Nature had made them impatient and withdrawn, with tendencies toward savagery and violence. Their legs had transformed into disquieting poles or harpoons. Their women's faces were covered with black shawls.

A dangling feeling of pity for the men's daily humiliation roused my sympathy. Guilt came to me like a bolt of lightning in the dark and fired my brain. In a lucid vision, a ghost appeared to me as a bee, reminding me to kneel down, to show the men and their boisterous women more kindness. My vision, which threatened to call me to the land of my forgotten ancestors, unfolded in a fantastic way. First there was an arbitrary knock at the door of the small house where I was sitting with the fishermen and their wives drinking the atrocious beverage. Next, a young man named Jowi, who had earlier presented his sad and yet humorous story to the gathering, fainted in his chair.

Jowi was a waif, an orphan who had no family nor friends. Every night he dreamed of a dead ancestor who read him his family tree from a gigantic book. This book contained the original faces of everybody on earth before their bodies were erased by the oceans and the whims of the sun. It catalogued the history of every family, and all forests, animals, plants, stones, types of metals, archipelagos, bacteria, insects, deaths, babies who died at birth, people who were raped, chairs, buildings, wars, conquests, kings, queens, chauffeurs, cleaners in hospitals, beggars. The book was God's register. It had an infinite number of pages and was so huge and wide, stretching from one side of the galaxy to another, that it took sixty thousand and eight young and strong-willed men to turn its voluminous pages.

The next morning I confessed my fears and disillusionment to Mollie. I didn't like the sea. I didn't like the harbour. I hated everything about the fishing boats. I detested the kinetics of floating on a flimsy vessel made of wood away from land and sanity, towards a demented ocean filled with crazy mermaids and sharks. I told Mollie what I felt. Going out to sea on a dinghy or boat to fish felt to me like heading straight to insanity. There was already enough insanity on land. It was pointless to go out to sea to look for more.

"Abandoning this project now, Mxolisi, will do you no good," Mollie said in a low voice, "but give it some time for the men to get used to seeing you around." I was a bit annoyed with Mollie's optimism. No self-respecting fisherman there would let anyone come an inch closer to his dinghy. I had spent hours on end conferring with the senior men in the group of fishermen Mollie had introduced me to. They didn't trust me. I heard one of the women calling Mollie a skollie from Cape Town. Clearly, most of the fishermen had no respect for Mollie. They hated him. They said he had come to Swartkops only to put a stop to their fishing business. "This man talks about fishing quotas all the time. How can we feed families from ten sardines per catch, two loaves of bread from spazas?" they complained loudly.

One particularly irate fisherman had denounced the abhorrent system of fishing quotas proposed by the government, "Phantsi ngezi layisensi zikarhulumente! Phantsi ngezikota zobubhanxa! Phantsi!" (Down with their useless fishing licence! Away with those mindless quotas!), he exploded, then quickly excused himself from the meeting to go to the public toilets.

Mollie gave me a soft smile that showed me that he understood my decision, and without saying anything more, started his Toyota Hilux bakkie, and drove away from Bhlawa.

28

It's 1.30 a.m. I'm woken up by a large contingent of police. They scream their sirens for some long minutes, use a very noisy loudhailer before I finally wake up. I am scared. Can't figure out quickly what is happening. Only the girl who lives sometimes in our small flat in Ntshekisa seems to be troubled by the attack. She is a tiny creature who is easily frightened by the characters lining Madala Street. We are living in desperate times, when people loot gold teeth from sleeping corpses. The policemen are shouting outside for the gates to be opened. "We are the police!" A neighbour who strolls the streets at midnight to smoke his cigarettes had seen two boys carrying my bakkie canopy towards Dora Street, and called the police. Luckily for me the police responded and apprehended the boys. Once cornered, they abandoned the heavy load and disappeared into the black streets. The canopy is now fixed securely to my bakkie. It is safe for now.

Yesterday Noxolo asked me to accompany her to Spar in Algoa Park. I stayed behind sitting on a bench while she went inside the shop. After a short while my eyes opened, and I noticed a young coloured girl, she must have been about 17 or 18, with three small kids, of 4 to 6 years crouching there in a corner outside the shop. She was sitting comfortably on the concrete pavement, her three agile kids were running around her, scantily dressed. The girl kept calling out to people who were returning from the shops with their groceries. I couldn't hear what she was saying, but there was always a bright smile on her face, her eyes ever glinting and so full of hope. She was a friendly girl, a kind soul, innocent, powerless, starving with her three kids. One guy, who apparently knew her plight, had bought her a takeaway. He gave it to her with two hands, almost praying softly. The girl smiled back a sunny smile. She went back to her sitting spot. The kids ran back and crowded around her, waited for her to open the takeaway and share the food with them. Like any kind mother, the girl took small bits and shared with the kids. The one kid jumped up, food in his one hand, lifted his other tiny hand and waved at the stranger who had bought their family some supper.

Last night after I arrived home, Noxolo told me a teenage boy and girl had been caught on camera by a neighbour having sex in the public park right next to our flat in Ntshekisa Street, in full view of everyone – children coming from primary school, parents walking in the street and motorists in their cars. The neighbour was so upset by the incident that he decided to share it in our neighbourhood WhatsApp group. Noxolo was outraged, "These little idiots are up to their tricks again. At first they break into our house. They are making a fool of everyone, including God. But he can see through their cunning." Just then a loud alarm sounded outside. Noxolo jumped up from the bed. The lower pane in the window had shattered. A red brick, apparently thrown with furious intent, had landed on the chair next to where I was standing.

On another occasion we heard the banging of a door outside the house. A woman with a ruptured voice was yelling loudly, "I wish they roast you in hell!" A boy with a knife had just robbed her of all her money.

One starry night I saw ten blind men dancing in a ring. The middle man, who was taller than the rest, was singing, bellowing, hard-done by the squalor and labour that men carry inside their chests. I quickly put on the feather hat that a boy stuck out to me in anger and started to walk towards my drunken world in Bhlawa. I could see that the beggar with one eye would certainly die one day, clinging to all his life's complex relationships, his unspoken seashells and looming agonies.

I stood waiting outside a Greenacres fish and chips shop. There was no one around. Why did I wake up so early to come here? I was wearing the crimson jacket and foolish red tie of the ghetto communist. I could hear music from somewhere, Nomzamo pouring her naked soul out to the world. I still held the gloomy hope that nothing was irrevocable, that forgiveness for our hostile world was possible. While I could never hope to live out my days in a new country with a dizzy horizon, I could still dream of a better race of people, of nostrils and eyes with no scars or blemishes.

29

I rear chickens for a meagre living in Mandela Park, Motherwell township. Sometimes I get frustrated by an open window of my chicken house and the wind charging the doors vehemently. Last night I sat in my room and read books. When I tired of their tumult, I sat alone outside the yard and contemplated the sea behind the spaza shop. I looked up again at the daunting sky. The houses near the penumbra of the moon were heavy with coffins. The activities of mourning and burial of the dead in the sea were lumped together with their skeletons.

The pandemic has been eating my chicken business in Motherwell. It has already swallowed up all the welders and the bricklayers. Just the other day I met Gladman, the fisherman. He told me there is no more snoek in Swartkops. Even the fish have abandoned the sea.

I need a buyer for my chickens fast. So I had little choice about meeting Molana and the tall woman who runs the frozen fish and chicken shop. I meet her assistant Claudine at the shop, a brisk girl, full of energy, who speaks straight with a kind voice. I feel suddenly loved and safe around her. As I step outside, I see two black men jump over a palisade fence, quickly remove a canopy from a bakkie parked in front of the butchery across the road. I wonder if I'm dreaming because it's exactly what happened to me. They lift it high on their shoulders and haul it over the high wall of the shopping complex to a waiting guy who stands on the street to receive it on his shoulders.

While this is happening, two men with green berets ask to see my permit for selling chickens during stage five of the lockdown. Residents are not allowed to be on the streets. Everyone has to stay indoors because of the pandemic. I turn around to look behind the workers' quarters where I had parked my botsotso bakkie. A young boy of not more than 14 years, is bending over its opened bonnet, removing the battery.

The email from Molana says I must deliver chickens to a farm in Draaifontein. I don't know the place. I don't trust the woman nor Molana, who is my contact. I might have seen the tall woman from a distance at the chicken shop (also known as the sawdust shop) in Greenbushes. She was reading from a book on a tripod stand in front of her. She sat on a high-up chair, glasses slanted over her dark eyes. She looked terribly unhappy. The sawdust shop was a bleak hell on earth. Inside you meet all kinds of characters, gnomes who plant poor seeds in the soil and want to escape the world to the nether places of the devil, doctors who carry large spatula spoons in their grey hands and are obsessed with measurements and flying drones, girls in blue shawls busy searching for lovers amongst the crowded animal feeds and moth-infested aisles.

I've reached the end of the road with the tall business woman. I fear my business will suffer permanently if I continue to supply chickens to her shop. Despite my reservations I doggedly grind on the next months supplying her. On the tenth month I write a WhatsApp message to show my disapproval with the little money she gives me for my chickens. Her last payment was extremely low, R26 per kilo. Molana strips my chickens to the bones. He skins them, puts away the gizzards, necks, feet, heads, livers, intestines, it's only after that that he weighs them. Then he says "Here Nkolisi. I give you this much for your chickens. They are too small." I don't enjoy my fights with Molana and the business woman. I make up my mind to leave them and their sordid business. I was never a part of their world. I go back to the township to plan my next move. I come back from Draaifontein very late, drained, still with no money. My negotiations with Molana and the woman to get my price for a kilo have failed.

Only yesterday I took two of my 2,5kg chickens to sell to Dolla, who had promised me to pay the R160 cash. I came to his place in Red Location, stood outside the gate because of the pandemic raging. At first I couldn't recognise the house. There were high walls marked with green snatches of old paint. A brand new wooden door straight from CashBuild had just been installed as an impediment to lost visitors. I stood outside the CashBuild door and shouted Dolla's name in the night. A door slowly opened, and from inside the black house a woman's head started to emerge. "Molo Sisi, which one is Dolla's house? Do you know Dolla?" The figure at the half-door twitched a little to one side, crouched low then disappeared from view. Then Dolla's voice replied, "Here Xi, it is me! Come inside Mxolisi, don't stand there."

Inside Dolla's house there were mannequin dummies, large dolls with broken fingers, satchels and wooden sculptures standing all around, seemingly guarding the place. Dolla leaned on the table and studied me closely. "Did you bring the chickens?" Before I could say anything his hands quickly took the two chickens in my cooler box and in one swift movement stashed them inside the fridge. Turning to me now slowly, Dolla told me he had already used up the R160. He asked for my Capitec bank account. He promised he would pay me come month end.

This morning I am waiting in a queue at the Magistrates Court in Bhlawa after receiving a court summons. I had opened a case for fraud and stock theft against Rasta, who was working for me, looking after my chickens in Motherwell. Two months ago he stole fifteen chickens, and also defrauded my customers. After I had caught him, he packed up his bags and left without notice. He then went to my customers to extort money they owed me, on the pretext that I had sent him. A police lieutenant advised me to go to the Small Claims Court to lay charges.

Death and mischief are palpable at the Magistrates' Court. Lawlessness walks through the long corridors sober as daylight, unashamed. Last night on the TV news I heard our housing minister say our country is immoral. "The courts and hospitals refuse to serve immigrants." He charged that the residents of Bhlawa have become xenophobic. "And yet," he says, "Zimbabweans and Zambians supported the freedom struggle." People are fighting for land, yet there are abandoned farms out there, doing nothing. Every day there are campaigns and banners in the streets. Ghosts of Poqo are fighting a war against the tsotsis of land in parliament.

The small crowd of men and women picketing on the lawn is getting rowdy. The leader of the demonstration says, "You don't have to go to law school to protest about your rights. Before you argue your case with the magistrate, look at the Bill of Rights and read sections 49 and 51." Inside the Magistrates Court dead people and wanton spirits are arguing about politics. Here outside in the yard I am next to a dejected man whose house has been taken over by his grandchildren. He tells me they want to throw him out into the street.

I hear fantastic tales that our future life in the township is looking very promising. One guy had read in the community newspaper *Isolabantu* that just across from his RDP house, a highway was going to be built to ferry manganese and platinum to the new Coega Harbour near Motherwell. It was said that the coming infrastructure projects in Bhlawa would create over a million jobs for the residents.

Someone in the queue tells an old woman that next year she won't have to chew hard on umleqwa and goat meat with her worn out false teeth. There won't be any need for that as you will be enjoying the soft and tenderized Streetwise2 KFC chicken, and downing this savoury meal from Kentucky in the USA with coleslaw and Coke. While we are sitting and imagining all sorts of rosy scenes about our future in Bhlawa, I suddenly start to sweat profusely all over my body with a strange fever, though it is bitterly cold inside the dreadful building of lawyers and angry thieves.

I begin to panic about the merit of my case. I'd often heard from my friend Sticks, who works as a delivery boy in a law firm in town, that the law favours the thieves. The lawyer handling my case tells me that dockets disappear all the time. "Cases are killed before the magistrate hears them." I'm sure this is what will happen to mine. Rasta believes strongly in witchcraft and uses iyeza religiously. He and his inyanga will make my docket invisible to the police and the lawyers. A young lawyer is shouting to a girl who wears high heels "Don't tell me lies. Start addressing me properly as Mr Bhuli. All protocols must be observed!"

The schoolboy who talks in riddles like a preacher says to his friend, "Do you know what that means?" The boy is dressed in his grey and white school uniform. His schoolbag is on the ground in front of his feet. The heavy bag is stacked on the floor like a small Table Mountain.
"They must leave Mampara alone," the schoolkid retorts sharply for everyone sitting on the bench, "can't they see that Mampara is crazy?"
Mampara is the homeless man who set parliament on fire in Cape Town. He has been throwing more tantrums from his prison cell. He wants an electric kettle and a stove in his cell. And a TV, so that at night he can watch the *Real Housewives of Cape Town*, his favourite soapie.

His lawyer battles to explain his behaviour.
"He rolled himself into a ball on his cell floor and refused to get up."
"He won't come to court today."
"Nobody cares about his rights."
"He is too weak to stand up."
"Last night he embarked on a hunger strike."
"He is in a poor state."
"The police must catch the big fish and leave Mampara alone."

Meanwhile a judge visits the defamed arsonist who is now a celebrity. Children can see what burns their dreams to ashes. A TV camera shocks the world and gives the children's miserable lives an overwhelming sadness.

30

These days I think a lot about the old people who died in Bhlawa in the 60's and 70's, forcefully driven out of their homes in Walmer, Korsten, South End, to be dumped in the black locations, some in Red Location and Veeplaas, others outside town, in Ciskei and Transkei, the Xhosa people's bantustans. My mind has been swimming in a haze, not caring to look at the nightmarish details of our history. I don't know what I've been thinking really. I need to discuss things with Sximba. Mzi is out of town. He has gone to a church in Lagos, to pray for our township.

I've also been feeling the meaninglessness of my decision to stay put while everyone is moving away. I try to phone Sximba to help me make sense of my dilemma, unlike me he has a warm view of life and people. Sximba's cell goes to voicemail. I get upset. Thoughts come from every direction and crowd in my head. Sximba's humble demeanour sometimes gets in the way and obscures the fact that his pride is big. He almost chased me away the day I asked him to join me, to work with me in the container.

I go to Sximba's place in Khwaza Street. I meet his cousin sister at the door. A white yapping puppy greets me on the outside stoep, looks me up and down, gives me another long look, distrusting my shabby appearance, and quickly loses interest. Sximba finally comes out of the garage where he keeps his working clothes, paints and canvases. The garage also serves as a home for his pigeons. On the stoep, scattered in long rows are bags of white, green, red and yellow grains of chicken feed, the kind you buy from Boxers stores. I can see that Sximba has been feeding his pigeons. He is dressed in his blue overalls and has a pair of gloves in his hands.

Sximba is in his usual reticent mood. I don't know how to approach him when he chooses to be silent. Maybe I have been too hasty. I tell him that I have come in peace. There's a big brown suitcase behind the door, where Sximba stores his old paintings. He goes towards the suitcase and sits heavily on top of it. It is completely dark inside the garage. There are no windows. One must spend a good deal of time inside, more than thirty minutes, to be finally able to see a human face, the outline of the toolbox, the pigeons' nest, a chair, a broken table, or the garden rake.

Houses in the township are not built like the ones that you see in the spacious city. They have the troubled shape of human faces. An invisible demarcation line splits a building right in the middle into two houses. Imagine a human face cut by a butcher's knife into two halves, each with one nostril, one dumb cheek, one eye and one ear. The brain is also halved in the process and you get two half-humans, one living in the one house, the other confusedly occupying the second house. The garage in Sximba's house lies right between two such disfigured, scarred and monstrous faces. The one face is looking east, and the other, Sximba's, instead of facing the opposite direction, west, is positioned obliquely at a wrong angle, exactly ninety degrees, placed heedlessly by the gods of apartheid to face south, pointing gingerly towards the Northern areas with their atrocities.

A door at the back end of the garage leads you to a tiny

passage towards the kitchen. The front door leads to Sximba's garden where he plants sunflowers, rosemary, white dandelions, some carrots and spinach. I am always puzzled about my exact bearings when I'm inside the garage. Disorientation happens like I'm being pushed inside a spinning earth that has no geography. I always feel that to avoid getting injured inside the garage, a first time visitor must be given a tiny map to mark his path. A cell phone torch is also useful to ward off the hungry spirits of the mysterious building. I doubt a wasp ever entered the building. The builder must have got all the measurements wrong. He built a storage house to keep family heirlooms and Sximba's pigeons.

Sximba sits on his brown suitcase looking pained with everything. He looks entirely distracted, like a dying man. The white puppy doesn't stop grunting and making funny sounds. I continue talking to Sximba in the dark. I sense he has stood up from the brown suitcase and is moving steadily towards me. I hesitate for a minute, doubting his location. I alter my position slightly and talk in the direction of his approaching shadow. I tell him again about my exciting proposal of ukuskopisa, advancing credit to our customers from the spaza shop in Motherwell. I desperately need someone I trust to help me in the business. Sximba stands next to me. Our foreheads almost touch. I can discern the outline of his face. He doesn't look too impressed. I offer him a monthly pay of nine hundred rands. He rejects my offer curtly saying he runs his own office from home. What he says leaves me so confused and I stay away from him for some weeks. I phone him the following month to apologize for talking in haste. I tell him I still want us to work together.

I consulted an igqirha woman about my problems. She started her treatment by telling me stories of our origins. She said that when people first walked on earth they could not see the worn out faces of the vengeful spirits, called iShologu, that were already there, nor hear the spirit of the trees. They were wandering bodies, like the minstrels of old, beggarly in appearance, seer-like creatures of the cold winds. Their ghoulish smell was sharpened by the spells of rivers and wailing forests. Inquisitive men and women spoke among themselves and decided to summon the commander of all life, uQamata. They walked the infinite space of darkness across the windless deserts to reach the tumultuous townships. After long months they arrived at new surroundings with different people. Music was played every day to attract good fortune, and to accelerate the physical motion of walking on stones. People listened to the wind. When Uko sang – Uko, the crying spirit who wandered all night moaning for the dead – the ill-fated artists picked up their guitars and joined in with a song of the struggle: "Nants' indod' emnyama Verwoerd, Basop' nants' indod' emnyama Verwoerd. Baleka nants' indod' emnyama." (Here comes the black man, Verwoerd. Look out, here comes the black man. You'd better run, the black man has arrived.)

The music came from open graves. It was the music of burning forests, black leopards and kudus fleeing to the roof of the world with careful teeth and horses' legs. That was a lonely artist's first composition, a song of rejoicing and moaning. He sang of bleeding hymens and burning evenings. His hungry mouth and red lips resembled the horrifying wounds of the seven seas. People laughed at his feet as if they were syphilitic. His songs flowed like tombs

142

to rivers and mountains. The gentle spirit of Mamlambo (river woman) rose up a level higher on the surface of the bent thorn. Her luminous eyes of the forest were fixed on death's door. The symbol of a god on her chest exploded the tiniest vertebrae of sniffing grass.

In the igqirha's second story an ostrich arrived at the front door of a bent house and met a stranger. The stranger was a man with a glum look, walking without shoes, who was later seen embracing a dead woman. A motherless goat went out of the front door and claimed the frozen bodies of dead sleepers, their skeletal corpses devastated. Two sisterly ghosts, ihlombe and inkenqe, arrived in the township. Black winds sailed through the stale air of amagqirhas' seances. Night songs drowned everyone with the tearless blood of running horses.

The igqirha's third story was about the road and its secrets. She said the amaXhosa people always speak of the long road of the rainbow as a cunning animal or a wandering night spirit, iHlola, which links the worlds of humans and immortal souls in the same way as the angel Gabriel guards the gates of heaven. The night spirit gave the black people passage to other worlds, but also invited chaos and death to their township – the increased instability of visiting strangers, doubtful ideas, belligerent police and soldiers. Like the hangman's noose iHlola has two ends, one often seen and felt by human hands and the naked eye, the other distant, somewhere in the infinite horizon, hidden from view.

She said a traveller must beg or ask for passage through a road before embarking on his journey: "Mandicel' indlela."

(I request permission to go and start my journey). When the traveller reached a certain point in his journey, he had to throw a stone nearby to mark a spot or a particular place of his own choice and interest. This place, called iSivivane, was a place of stones, affirming acceptance of a traveller by his ancestors and divine guidance during his passage in life. When it came to the liberation of poor people from apartheid, the second end of the road, iHlola wrung the necks of black children who came out of the township to a land of ghosts and vicious animals. They could not trust what the rainbow said to them. In the rich town they met highwaymen who implored them to stay. Because they were hungry they remembered how to fear, for they were visitors from the world of the poor. On the seventh day in the rich town they were called to a big feast. And when it was their turn to recite the usual greeting and learn not to be doubtful anymore, they once more witnessed the soundless death of the faraway roads.

After the igqirha woman's stories about how the world was created by Umdali, she exclaimed, "Vuma!" and I answered, "Ndiyavuma". When the sea heaved I heard her voice sounding boldly from the compromised stars: "Mxolisi, the longer you remain in the waters, the further you walk away from everyone. The further you walk away from yourself, the deeper the sea within you grows. Vuma!"
I answered, "Ndiyavuma."
"Vuma!"
"Ndiyavuma."
In her white and blue robes she continued, "Come, hear what the sea has to say for itself, what the three winds contest – and the three moons! Come and hear death's trampling on the tarmac, telling us that a bull must be slaughtered

to appease abaphantsi. And that the big animal that is desperate must be sacrificed for peace. Listen carefully Mxolisi when the sea calls you, when it calls your name!"
This woman of the winds then took me to the sea to breathe. I held her hands. We went to the sea to get a bath from the pool of human tears.

31

Sximba appeared in the evening TV news last night. He had won a writing prize and lots of money. I visited him the following morning at his house and found him still sleeping. He told me he had been out most of the night to celebrate his win with a few of his friends.

After inquiring about a few odds and ends, I came to the crux of my visit, to advise him to get married. "Bear in mind Sximba, you won't stay young forever. A wife is a special person. She will take good care of you even in your old age. But as our culture dictates, you must show her family that you deserve her. She will keep your house warm, bear you lots of children. Go and pay lobola to your future in-laws. Be wise and use your earnings ngendlela. Do you know Satch, Dolla's famous brother of the hit-song *Oh Chacklas Chacklas*? Satch told me that one day a very wise old woman here in Bhlawa warned him, 'Sukubophelela imali yakho epipini mntanam! (Do not wrap all your hard-earned cash around your penis my child!)' "

Yesterday I walked to the middle of a temple in Ntshekisa street, near my home. I looked around. There were flowers and chairs. There was a door. Behind the door a window, and a man standing. Staring at nothing. There was an indecipherable sound that appeared to come from the derelict whorehouses of the dead. A poem or a song was being recited by children. It was the same song we used to sing when I was six years old.

noposi uvela phi
noposi uvel' ebhayi
ndizomxelel' utat' omncinci
uhamba ngomlenz' ogoso

pikinini nobhalana
pikinini nobhalana
is a child's song for the postman

wee pikinini nobhalana
wee pikinini nobhalana
a child sings for the old man

she hears the dreadful news –
a strong bird will fly in the wind
children will follow the sun
the world will spin in the wind

pikinini nobhalana
pikinini nobhalana
the birds know the postman
children must follow the birds

noposi uvela phi
noposi uvel' ebhayi
ndizomxelel' utat' omncinci
uhamba ngomlenz' ogoso

mr. postman, where do you come from
mr. postman, you come from ebhayi
i will tell my uncle
you walk with a broken leg

men ride their bicycles
women walk
men ride their bicycles
children walk to school

my father rides a bicycle to work
my mother walks to the hospital
a chronicle of mothers and birds

Next to the balustrade stairs of the hollowed out temple was a man who sat on a chair surveying the universe. He saw everything that was happening in the township, even the alarming worlds of the police and amagqwirha. He opened a book with scrawny fingers, a book which contained everything. It was conceived of stones and was covered in his own blood.

I thought more about the fishermen. They were living abnormal lives. I didn't know how they managed it. Either early in the morning, or very late in the evening they went out and visited death in its castle. They were happy about it and always talked about bringing in a big haul of sardines or oomasbhanka. I could never understand their blasé attitude about the dangers of the sea. They were forced to invent new ways of escaping death every time they arrived at the ocean. The lure of the sardines was probably too much for them. They were like prisoners who went back to their jail cells in order to break free again. The routine of begging the sea was the same as begging on land – a squashed sailor's cap in one hand, a harpoon, a fishing vessel, a dinghy or boat, fishing bait, a horrible net. The same equipment as the beggars use in our township.

The fishermen study the seas. They look out for any trace of life, a tiny movement or a flimsy disturbance to the gentle sea, under the water. The fish move around like men and women inside a shebeen, or a married couple in their RDP house in the township. The female fish says to her husband: "The house is lovely. And our children will soon be born. We will apply from SASSA for the children's grant. You, my lovely husband, will soon abandon me with your five boys when you've had enough of me. You will go out and look for a fresh and younger woman, a lithe yellow bone with a supple body. You will break her down too with your charm, conquer her young body. You swore long time ago that you will work for no man. The government's R350 grant will suffice for all of us in our home. It will clothe us, provide medicine, send the children to school, buy their books and uniform, bring us grocery from the spaza shop, buy paraffin when the weather is too cold, pay our taxi fares, feed your concubines."

The fisherman waits outside, above the surface of the sea, howling for attention from the fish. He throws out his fishing line with a wriggling worm harpooned on its hook. The sardine looks up and sees everything. The fisherman howls louder and louder begging the sardine to open its mouth and take the bait.

32

Everywhere I went demons and singing spirits followed me, even through crowds of onlookers, or when walking past old men standing by their front gates looking at the defiant world. These beings followed me through sleep and waking like obstinate beggars. I never had a chance to own anything, not a horse nor a blundering soul. I wrote everything on the wall in the spindly shapes of mathematics. To ensure that my teachers never abused my performance of numbers and visible orbits of stars, I showed them the numbers that I had programmed in my soul. Trees, animals, songs, seamen's tales were my friends and enemies. They gave me tortuous times. They were like long prisons, sad butterflies, black spades. I ended each day by walking to the ocean to look for the mermaids and the drinking seafarers.

Something within me showed me the black satin which covered oblivion. I grew uncomfortable with the haunting beauty of dead town in the evenings. I did not know what was left to share with the dead spirits who owned the harbour, nor the meaning of their ships which suddenly forgot their human cargo. I hardly slept. I did not mind the affairs of the rich women who stood happily at the harbour like a hundred sirens, wearing pink shoes, on their way to distant lands. The devil was a lonely woman who cut her clean nails in teary anguish. But that evening at the harbour in dead town, I admired the black sea.

One night a procession of thieves and mongrels commenced

walking from the Holy Virgin Mary, right up Church Street towards the mayor's office in dead town. Slithering snakes and green reptiles took over the building. Inside the chamber guileless councillors were sweating under a table, counting their steps to a gully in the middle of a street where their souls were going to be laid to rest. The rest of the community folded their tents and left. The township grew into an oven burning with human skulls. The voices of two children mimicked the wily roads and prayed religiously to the charcoal face of God.

There was a house in Mendi Street where Milambo, the spirit of death, entered through the chimney. He came from the underworld with twenty pounds of flesh, wounds on his chest and the ill-fated rump of a thikoloshe. He brought with him the vulgarity of women. Whispers of the dead were heard every night in all the rooms. Evil ghosts in the house had packed Milambo's human remains in an antiquated chamber sealed with tape. Although this house carried many scandals, it was never demolished by the government. Directly beneath it, close to a taxi rank near a slum with gruesome doves, lived prostitutes with fresh scars. In that slum kingdom there were opposing kings who oppressed the wings of the dying. My walk always took me past the haunted bioscope which ran the movies of the dead constantly, one gory film after another. In a nearby house, in a street just opposite the whorehouse, lived a boy who had murdered his mother.

I knew that beyond that darkness and smog there was earth, light and freedom. There were people like me who thought and felt like I did. The earth, though I could not see it from my room in Madala, was round like a rolling ball. The moon was white like the sea. Nothing was invisible except water, earth, wind and fire, those four elements. God was the fifth element. He watched us and said nothing.

There was a fatal accident on Ferguson Road, a gruesome collision of a blue Corolla with a Quantum taxi resulting in fifteen lives lost, including four babies.

"Do you think her head was raised to the left when the car hit her?" the man who sells lamps whispers in a frenzy to a woman vegetable hawker. The woman with sad eyes answers back in her sonorous voice. Just then a stranger with a stern look joins their conversation. The lamp seller is convinced that an evil spirit was involved. He starts blustering out, "I dreamt this accident last night. In my dream three families were bickering in the taxi while the owner of the taxi was calling for calm. But a stubborn young woman wanted the driver to overtake all the cars in the road. She was waving her arms at the driver all the time, getting him mixed up with a past lover who dumped her with a baby while she was at school, ezilalini in Peddie." The plump woman and the tall stranger listen attentively to the pedlar of bedroom lamps.

"Do you think it is witchcraft?" the stranger asks.

"Of course. Only a powerful witch can kill so many people at one time," the man replies.

This horrific accident was the usual dirty business of death in the township. Someone suggests that a cow must be slaughtered by the residents to appease the dead people of this dangerous road. Another says a bloodthirsty snake lives underground in Ferguson Road, a nkanyamba snake that mines the busy road for human souls and their blood. Nobody really knows why a silent killer visits such callous devastations on the lives of people here. Smacking its big lips, the unrestrained spirit of thikoloshe lifts up the skirts of little girls. It poisons the throat of the hunchbacked widow who stays alone in a house in Gqamlana, watching the world with frightened eyes.

A heavy smog spews from Carbon Black, the chemicals factory in Deal Party, and suffocates our lungs. It is a huge and impassable obstacle at night, deepening the shadows of prowling spirits and invisible thieves. Next to it there is a waste treatment plant, so that every night the stench of human waste surrounds the township like a sentinel, bringing us emphysema and asthma. The havoc that is caused to our sleep at night by the smell of shit spills over into the day. It manifested itself in women's tears. One day a woman who was weeping at her table provoked a panic of curiosity among other women for her bluish tears which had a sweet and granular taste. The shit smell caused all forms of hallucinations and dangerous behaviour. It led to peaceful families suddenly becoming violent and breaking up. It was surmised by the residents that phosphorous fumes from the stench damaged the nerves.

Songs sung by invisible spirits followed me wherever I went in the dirty streets and all over the township slums. The empty revelries and excessive drinking habits of people in the township amongst all the chaos of the police and the squalor never failed to bewilder and torture my mind. My friend Shepherd still lived in Chris Hani making his linocuts and wire sculptures. A white businessman brought a busload of curious tourists to his art studio. Their presence at the squatter camp caused him to drink more heavily and eventually he lost his mind.

The ghostly father will return to the grieving altar hoping for a miracle. The earth and the dwarfed god of sunrise hide their militant anguish. I was born blind and wanting with the long night whistles and sad biological malice. In the deceptive garden the rose tree blooms and gives the roads ancient knowledge and animal blood. It gives exultant pain to a soul that fires like the plagues of Egypt, swallowing pesticides, breaking miscarriages. Thus I arrived in the world inside two ships with no carriers or numbers, repeating fury and velocity.

I sometimes come across an igqirha woman who stands in the sea and sways her entire body in a circle, calling out to an invisible presence below the surface, swirling the sea waters with the circular movement of her hands. She gently lowers onto the tide a bottle of brandy and a small plate with tobacco and a match, they sail out to be swallowed by the sea, to be received by the hands of abaphantsi. The woman of the winds turns her back to the ocean. Sometimes her hands drag towards the shore a mother goat. She picks up a knife and slaughters the animal and gives a libation. Having seen the unfolding of a different world I have enough grief for a funeral. I turn my back against the ocean and leave.

33

My father worked hard in his life of 68 years, smoking his Van Ryn's cigarettes, looking after my mother, myself and my three brothers. We always had books at home which my mother bought through *Reader's Digest*. But it took me quite a long time to realize the magnificent power of written words, especially poetry. To respect and adore words for the heroic beings and angels they are, often frequenting our despairing souls with the softness of their breath.

When I started writing I gave everything to my head to process and to find a formula. My head was working furiously doing the background work, conscious of its deadline. Attuned to the clockwork of time, it was enjoined to infinity and was precise. My head communicated its findings and made recommendations. Nothing could go wrong. My head was detached from the rest of my body, disinterested in people. I had no motor connections and no visible ambition. I was an expert in my line of work, which was arranging air. I worked like a certified researcher. No, not a researcher: I took dictation, I was the secretary! I had never met my head, my boss. I didn't even know what he looked like. But I was loyal and tried to follow the fly around my room.

The office was a small space surrounded on all sides by emptiness and the bored reek of lonely green files. I took everything from the shelves, papers, files and memories one at a time, passed every tiny bit over to my head to consider. My head was patient with the world and folded everything away, approximated the century for the hard results. This was methodical work in an invisible world. My head knew what my head was doing. My head knew what my body was doing. Everyone knew everything. Don't ever believe them when they say otherwise. Everything was spontaneous, must always be spontaneous. Nothing was final. My head loudly instructed me to breathe air. It was always past midnight, past our sleeping time.

I always look at the world through my window in the township. Little has changed. The houses built by the municipality in a street near the beer hall are falling down. The law in the township jungle is greedy and violent. Everything I see I condemn. I judge harshly. I compare the world to my simple spot in this harbour. The shadow that hangs low over the docking ships and the dismal harbour, looks bloodless and cold like the fingers of the dead. I notice that the housefly only circles the food that I put on the table in front of me. It wants to partake of my meal, dine or die with me. It ignores the custard that has dripped down from my plate to smear the floor with its bright yellow colour.

There are two things on my mind as I write these words: Gentleness and sorrow. Sorrow and gentleness. I walk. I laugh. I cry. I saw a girl who was looking for a real world, searching for the road. I saw two men leaning against a hanging cliff. A brazen motor car driven by a smiling woman passed by. Next in the miserly queue stood a beggar with torn clothes. He too was looking for a green thread.

Almost every morning I go barefoot to the sea to look for poems. The sea is very close to where I live. I sometimes hear it laughing or shouting in the night. It seeps and dances along the shore for many miles. The mysterious water is blue or dark green and never fades from the looker's eyes. My body is the warm sternum of a flying fish, the busy wing of some faraway eagle. My torso and my limbs are enmeshed in a dark pact. My body exists as a coy ally, a friendly organism of feelings and actions. An insect, a bedbug, eats slowly at my flesh. I stand up to remove the shirt that hides the intruder. The insect goes and sits elsewhere. An alliance must begin for the entire world to serve my flesh and the inscrutable bug.

My teachers were superstitious. They taught me to read and write but paid scant attention to my jagged spirit. Their suicidal fears didn't bother me. Right from the start I was accused of writing bleak poems, using a metaphoric language which sought to confuse and did nobody any good. My detractors at school accused me of escapism and deception, of obscure feelings and extreme negativity. They said my poems danced out of the pages of my notebooks in confusion. I said nothing, because I had heard the poet's song. The poet's song is the road towards all those who went before us, who had to see the sun go down before their eyes. The poet's song is the anthem of those who laid down their lives. The ones who went unperturbed to the government and asked the prevaricators the whereabouts of freedom. My poems were my map and geography.

I continue to write my poems despite the sea's provocation. They struggle to sing. They are the silence and sky in the township. The space and fallow ground. They breathe inside me from slums wrecked by hatred. They are the drowning sounds of gasping mermaids below the sea. I walk every night in Bhlawa looking up at the falling sky.

In the rundown schoolyard dead birds prune their wings, their lives devastated. They sit and hoot on top of the long chimneys in the graveyard at Veeplaas, scaring everyone. They fly away from the harbour in a V-shaped echelon towards the red houses of Red Location.

I suppose even now, right at this moment, I am still struggling to talk to a reluctant world which never listens. Even in the deepest of silences in my bed when I'm alone or sleeping, I cannot hear myself. I look at the mirror in my room in front of me, and all I can see is a pitiful shadow. My poems are ways by which I try to hurry my struggle to speak. Something has been taken away from the world. Hearts? Dreams? Women? Dogs? I don't know. I am not so sure now of how the melodious winds drive their rhythm of insanity up my spine. Or how often the madman howls every other night, consumed by his hatred for life and his nightmares of the coming world. I hear the struggle of voices in bondage. If words do not quite fit, I look for music or I turn back to the writing of others to find what I am looking for. I will find them. I will just look more, think more about the harrowing life in Bhlawa.

I will always remember working feverishly in my room in Madala Street in the 80's, facing a whiteboard and working out algebraic equations, while outside the police were firing guns and shots randomly. Then followed the sounds of young feet running and jumping fences outside the yard, escaping the police and the soldiers. It was not because I was aloof to the suffering and the chaotic life in our township. I contributed to the struggle in my way. I was thinking and writing what will happen after. I was training myself to see.

34

In an eccentric house in a nameless street I saw God for the first time. He was talking to someone I had last seen years ago. That night it was Christmas, always a bad time of the year for presents. God was holding something in his hand, a dark blade or a corrupted file from the scriptures. The Gospel of Matthew was in the wrong place, first chapter. I did not greet God but I knew he was an enigmatic animal, a flying black bird, a burning sun. God was inspecting the world before deciding to leave us on a drifting boat to be lost eternally. The perpendicular sea harboured a resentment against the hearts of damned men. The perfect ocean turned a circular wave, caressing the pebble eyes of cruel wolves. I knew then that God was infinite.

I opened the door of the house very slowly. Outside the rain was falling heavily. Down the block other kids came out yelling, singing and dancing, "Sicel' iKhrismesi! Sicel' iKhrismesi!" (We ask for Christmas! We ask for Christmas!) I stepped out into the night, led bravely forward by a little blue light that seemed to come from a moving truck. In the cold township streets the world continued to follow me relentlessly like a conniving thief. Another year dragged its feathers into the black light, ready for a new orgy. The devil's music played, and the blue drums that bind invisible worlds together.

Our house which craved blue paint on its walls stood behind me. I was worn out, made slow by the massive strokes of history.

"Who are these people who hunger in the streets?"

"Where do they come from?"

"What gives you the right to talk on their behalf?"

The rain comes to our houses and falls over our skies with the same rhythm. The thief comes in the night to our homes and leaves – where to, nobody knows. I think about our mothers and grandmothers. My fingers buckle and pain turns them blue. My neck aches. There is everything wrong with the world. One beggar in one street, in another street a pauper collecting old metal and broken beer bottles. Someone once told me the story of the sea and its promiscuous seven daughters. The sea enables all our stories.

We carry the hefty price of freedom on our shoulders. We also want to do everything now, to decapitate the nightmares of our violent history with one blow. For Bhlawa, a township that has swum in a dark pit for so long, is such a feat possible? Nobody wants to know where poor people live, what they eat or don't eat, and how they die. In fact we have become accustomed to talking about poor people with such assertive fervour and wizardry of words that the poor have become appendages and shadows, devices to instantly anaesthetise our innermost feelings. The professional lie thrives in the new breeze.

The day my schoolteacher at Thembelihle gave me a zero mark for a writing assignment, that was the day I stopped dreaming of becoming a biology or chemistry teacher in a township school, and became a restless poet. Mr. Caper stood in front of the shocked and embarrassed standard ten class displaying the dreadful mark on my script – 0 – for all my classmates to see. I was a young boy with a calm temperament, but burning coals were already gathering in the furnaces of my soul. No one, not even my classmates, could feel its rising temperature.

One teacher asked, "Mxolisi, what would you like to grow up to be?" I answered without a pause, "A sweeper of streets and a polisher of men's shoes." I have not strayed that much from that. Every wish that I harboured secretively in my heart like a pebble has been kindly granted to me by the universe. What is there to worry about? I can sleep at night, and pray softly upon awakening in the morning. One summer's day I saw a blue seal dancing happily in the sea.

The dawn of democracy didn't mean anything to me. I had a poet's vision of the world, a skewed lens of a triangular vision. I had lived too close to death so very often that life and its supposed magnificent virtues and qualities astonished and frightened me. It was not easy to be a child. But Bhlawa in those days was more sunlight and sunrays than dereliction and squalor. The residents could manage their state of poverty. Poverty had made us all equal. When I look back at the interiority of our township lives, the liturgy of our oppression, its disorderly aura, I forgive myself for my bit of insanity.

Printed in the United States
by Baker & Taylor Publisher Services